ORYON

∞ ∞ ∞ ∞ ∞

M.K. Eidem

The Imperial Series

Cassandra's Challenge
Victoria's Challenge

Tornians

Grim
A Grim Holiday
Wray
Ynyr

Published by M.K. Eidem
Copyright © 2015 by Michelle K. Eidem
Cover Design by Judy Bullard
Edited by: www.bellamediamanagement.com
and
A-Z_Media@outlook.com

∞ ∞ ∞ ∞ ∞

I'd like to thank my family for all their support during this exciting time of my life, especially my husband. I couldn't have done it without you. I'd also like to thank all my friends that have been there for me, answering questions and helping guide me, Judy, Reese, Annie, Carol, Sally, Julie, Fern, Beth, Susan and Narelle. Thanks, ladies!

∞ ∞ ∞ ∞ ∞

Chapter One

Isis silently gazed out the open dome of their spaceship, the Hunter, watching as Betelgeuse grew larger. Goddess her home world was beautiful. A shining jewel in the blackness of space, guiding them home and she had never even realized it. All those years... and she had never seen what her world looked like from space. Why? She always wanted to. She would ask Oryon to bring her to this room the first few years after their Joining but something else had always been more important and she finally stopped asking.

Once a year, for over twenty-five years, she had been allowed to travel to Tornian with Oryon and be present to hear the Emperor's first address of the year to the Lords. That had occurred earlier this year with Emperor Wray presenting Kim, declaring her Tornian and making her his Empress, shocking everyone. The only other Assembly that females were allowed to attend was Joining Ceremonies like the one they had just left.

So this time, she hadn't asked. She had just left their chambers and opened the dome herself. Several warriors had given her strange looks as she passed, but no one stopped her. Why hadn't she done this years ago?

Reaching into her pocket, she pulled out the comm Empress Kim had given her, and she knew why she hadn't done it before. She hadn't considered it possible that a female could come and go as she pleased, that she had the *right* to do so. She knew better now, thanks to her... friends.

She now had females she considered friends and because of them she now realized there were a great many things she had the right to, like helping rule her House and there were things she had never thought possible... were, like her releasing while Oryon was Joined with her.

She wanted to do more than *sit* at Oryon's side as he'd allowed for the first time just the other day. She wanted to *stand* by his side and be a major part of his life, *their* life and help him rule Betelgeuse, not just be the female that gave him offspring.

Would he allow it? He had enjoyed the changes in their relationship since the Joining Ceremony. They now rested together every night, all night, whether they Joined or not. They kissed and it was amazing but Isis had learned after talking with Kim and Abby that there were even more amazing things they could do together. Things Isis wanted to try.

"Isis?" Oryon's quiet question had her turning to find the only male she had ever wanted, joining her in the room.

"Yes?" she asked.

"Why are you here?" he questioned. He had received dozens of frantic comms, detailing every step of his Lady's journey. None had known what to do when they'd seen her walking the corridors without him, nodding to them.

"Did you realize this is the first time I've ever seen Betelgeuse from space?" she asked, ignoring his question. Her gaze returned to the planet on the other side of the dome.

"What?" Oryon looked from her to their planet. "That can't be. We've returned home many times and..."

"And every time I asked you to bring me here, other things were always more important."

"That's not true!" Oryon denied, but thinking back he realized it was. Isis *had* asked during the first years of their Joining and he *hadn't* brought her. "Why did you not say something?"

"Would it have mattered?" she asked, already knowing the answer and Oryon snapped his jaw shut.

Oryon didn't know what to say. His Isis had changed so much in the last few weeks. Their *world* had changed and he was still trying to adjust. Never before would Isis have dared to venture out of their chambers alone. Never before would she have questioned him, not like this. Yet never before had he been so... satisfied. He and Isis were now resting together, every night. They shared kisses, special touches and meals together. Why had he never thought to do this before? Because he never thought she would allow it. Tornian females rarely had contact with their male outside of Joinings and then, only to tell him what they wanted in order to remain or they would leave him to Join with another male. Yes, Isis had been different, she actually spoke to him about their offspring and allowed him to touch her outside Joinings but she had never indicated she would desire more.

Now they ate meals together and he found he enjoyed them, enjoyed telling her about his day.

Now Isis would press her lips to his in that wonderful thing called kissing that they had learned about because of King Grim and his Queen and he enjoyed that too.

Now his Isis rested with him, every night. Waking to find her in his arms was... Oryon wasn't sure what it was, but he treasured it.

But it was her allowing him to touch her... whenever he wanted to and her returning that touch that he cherished the most. It excited, yet soothed him, at the same time. It felt right, it felt natural and he knew he could never live without it now. Especially not when so much else in their lives had changed. Ynyr, his third male had been chosen by the Emperor himself, to replace Bertos as Lord. To say Oryon had been shocked was an understatement. Isis had always told him that Ynyr was special, that he was more than what his manno saw, and she had been right.

She was the one that had insisted he send Ynyr to the Emperor for special training, so he could return to Betelgeuse to assist Oryon with the training of his warriors. Making House Rigel, the place all would want to send their young males for training.

Now Ynyr would be taking that training to Etruria where he would need every skill he had learned to repair the damage Bertos and Risa had caused and create his own House.

Ull, his first male, was struggling to come to terms with all that had happened. Ull hadn't been selected in the Joining Ceremony and while it had hurt his pride, he would have been able to overcome that since *no* male had been chosen. But then, Ynyr had been made Lord of one of the most important Houses in the Empire and an Earth female had chosen *Ynyr* as her male.

That Ull wasn't handling well, and Oryon knew that was partially his fault. Ull had never had to struggle the way Ynyr had. He had never truly understood what it felt like *not* to be a first male. Oryon did, for he had been his manno's second male and knew his place was to support his brother. It wasn't until his twentieth year, at the death of his brother in battle that Oryon had become next to rule.

Ull had always known that one day he would be the Lord, and because of that, he would have at least one female. He had never once had to doubt it, now he did.

"My Lord." Oryon turned to find his Captain behind him. "We are approaching Betelgeuse."

"I know that Shen," Oryon said impatiently, watching as Isis moved closer to the dome.

"I... yes my Lord," Shen stuttered surprised by the impatience in his Lord's voice. "But you always wish to personally supervise our arrival."

"Not this time Shen, take care of it."

"Yes my Lord." Giving Isis' back a quick look Shen bowed and left the room.

Oryon waited until Shen was gone before he moved to stand behind Isis. Slowly he reached around her touching a spot on the dome. "That is where our home is," he quietly told her, his lips grazing her ear as he spoke.

Isis raised her hand, slowly covering his fingers with hers, as she too touched their home. "There?" she asked softly.

"Yes," he said, curling his fingers to capture hers.

"It's beautiful," she breathed out, leaning back against his powerful chest.

"Not as beautiful as you are," he told her gruffly.

Tipping her face up, she found his lips a hair's breadth away and truth blazing in his amazing gray eyes. "You think I'm beautiful?"

"The most beautiful creature the Goddess ever created." He told her before capturing her lips for a hard kiss.

Twisting, Isis wrapped her arms around him returning his kiss, pulling him even closer.

"Goddess, Isis," Oryon groaned, his hands sliding down to grip her firm ass, grinding her against his throbbing shaft. He couldn't believe how quickly she could arouse him now. All it took was a touch, a look and he was ready to Join with her.

"Touch me Oryon," she begged, guiding one of his hands to her breast, squeezing it encouragingly.

"Yes!" he agreed taking it further by sliding his hand up, pulling down the sleeve of her covering revealing the glorious piece of flesh to his gaze. Leaning down he captured the taut, dusty nipple with his mouth, sucking on it the way he'd discovered drove her wild.

Stretching onto her toes, Isis offered him more. "More Oryon," she pleaded, feeling her channel flood and clench with need. Never had their previous

Joinings been like this. While they touched more and rested together, Oryon still pleasured her with his mouth first. Oral sex, as she had been informed by Kim and Abby, making her channel slick enough for him to enter her. Now, she knew her channel was already slick enough and she wanted him inside her, wanted to know if she could release while he was inside her the way Earth females could.

Reaching down she unfastened his pants, her hand slipping inside to grip his rock hard shaft, freeing him. This was something else she'd always wanted to do, but never thought possible, now she was going to do what seemed right, natural with *her* male.

"Isis!" Oryon gasped, ripping his mouth away from her breast in shock. Goddess, she'd never touched him like that before and his hips instinctively pumped into her hand. It felt amazing.

"I want you Oryon," Isis said raising dark eyes to his, letting him see her need as she tightened her grip. "Now! I need you inside me now!"

Oryon's mind was reeling. This was not the proper way to Join with his Isis. He needed to pleasure her with his mouth first, but his hands weren't listening. They were pulling her covering up and out of the way, lifting to brace her back against the dome while he positioned himself between her parted legs.

As the massive head of his cock nudged her entrance, its hot slickness had him pausing, as a moment of sanity returned. "Isis..." he began but before he could say more, the legs that were wrapped around his hips tightened, jerking his cock into the only place it wanted to be, deep inside her.

Gasping, Oryon slapped a hand on the dome. Goddess she was hotter and slicker than she'd ever been before and he couldn't stop himself from thrusting even deeper into her.

"Yes Oryon!" Isis cried out, gripping his shoulders as her hips rocked against him, her channel already tightening around him. "More," she demanded.

Oryon couldn't remember a time when he'd felt so out of control, not even during their first Joining when it had been *his* first time inside a female. That experience had altered his life, making him a male but this... this changed *everything*. His Isis wasn't just allowing him to take his pleasure, she was contributing to it, driving his pleasure even higher with each stroke and seemed to be receiving as much pleasure in return.

With every deep, pounding stroke, he swore she got tighter, squeezing him until suddenly she cried out, her walls tightening painfully around him. He could do nothing but roar, as he released inside her.

Oryon discovered his legs weren't the strong, steady ones he'd relied on all his life, as he fought to keep both of them upright. Never before had he experienced anything as magnificent as feeling his Isis releasing while he was inside her. It had made his own release more powerful, as if it had exploded from his very soul and he knew they were now Joined together for all eternity.

"My Lord!" The sound of his warriors rushing in to see why their Lord had roared caused Oryon's strength to quickly return. He quickly separated their bodies, making sure Isis was steady on her feet, before stuffing his still semi-hard shaft back into his pants. No one saw his Isis like this. She was his vision and his alone.

Spinning around, he found more than a dozen warriors had stormed into the observation room, their mouths dropping open as they took in the condition of their Lord.

"Why are you here?!!" Oryon demanded.

"My Lord," Warrior Shen spoke, his eyes flying to the reflection of Lady Isis in the dome as she fixed her covering, but not before he saw the luscious curve of her ass. "We heard your roar and thought you were calling for assistance."

"Since when do I need assistance when I am with my Lady?!!" Oryon growled angrily. "Leave! Now! Or you will all meet my sword!" His warriors stumbled over themselves obeying their Lord, Shen being the last to leave.

Oryon waited until he was sure they were alone before he turned back to Isis. His breath caught at what he found. Isis' forearms were pressed against her heaving chest. Her fists covered her lips, swollen from his kisses. Her face was flushed and tears leaked from her tightly closed eyes. Goddess what had he done? How could he ever make this right?

Then she did something he never expected, she opened her brimming eyes and started to laugh. A mirth filled laugh that had her eyes sparkling and a large grin breaking across her face.

"Oh Goddess, Oryon! Did you see their faces?" she asked gasping, tears streaming down her cheeks. "They really thought... that..." She found she couldn't go on. Goddess really? They'd known it was just her and Oryon in the room. There was no way she could ever harm him!

"You could you know," he said putting an arm on either side of her, caging her in between his hard body and the dome.

"Could what?" she asked still laughing, not realizing she'd spoken aloud.

"Harm me. You are the only one that could." His eyes were serious as they met hers.

"What?" she whispered her humor fading.

"You, Isis, are my one weakness. I would sacrifice everything for you, even my honor."

Isis' eyes flickered over the face she'd loved since she'd first seen it at the age of eighteen. He was even more handsome to her now, because now, she really knew him and he was a wonderful male. He was her male and she never wanted him to have to sacrifice anything. Reaching up she gently framed his face. "I would never ask that of you Oryon. I love you too much. I always have." Stretching up she gently kissed his lips.

"And I love you Isis," he murmured against her lips, his heart swelling at her words. "Come let us go home." Pushing off the dome, Isis caught the hint of a devilish smile on his lips, one that told her he was thinking of something particularly naughty.

"What are you thinking?" she asked.

"I'm thinking that we need to travel more, so I can show you Betelgeuse from space every time we return."

Isis felt her entire body flush at what Oryon was implying. "Next time we'll make sure we shut the door."

"And lock it." Oryon agreed leading her from the observation room, neither noticing the star that twinkled brighter for a moment.

Chapter Two

It was with new eyes that Isis' gaze traveled over her home, House Rigel. Its exterior was made from massive logs harvested centuries earlier, which formed thick, impenetrable walls. Stone boulders stood like silent sentries before a set of enormous doors. Sometime in the distant past, craftsmen had carved an intricate hunt scene into those doors, announcing to all what was expected of those that passed through them. As the doors opened, the immense fireplace welcomed the weary hunter and drove away the chill during the cold season.

House Rigel wasn't the magnificently elegant place that House Torino was. It was more relaxed and comfortable in a rough way, exactly what the House of a Hunter's planet needed to be. Males from across the Empire came here to hone their hunting and tracking skills, to prove they were worthy of being called a Warrior. Through those carved doors, generations of the Empire's greatest Warriors had passed, and it filled Isis with pride to know that *her* male was its Lord.

Frowning, she looked from the obvious places in the room to those that weren't so obvious. She had talked in depth to Lisa about what she had done within House Luanda about her openly displaying what King Grim had given her. About *how* she had gone about it, because Isis wanted to do the same thing here. She wanted House Rigel to shine just as brightly as Betelgeuse did in space and she now realized she had her work cut out for her.

This place definitely needed a female to make it shine. There was dirt in the corners, dirty equipment stacked against the walls and the windows weren't even clean. Her chambers would never be allowed to get in such a condition and neither would Oryon's. So why wasn't that same attention being given to the rest of the House? Well, she would make sure it was from now on.

"Isis?" Oryon's question had her eyes turning to him. She found Oryon along with all the males returning from Tornian with them watching her.

"Yes?" she asked.

"Is something wrong?" They'd been moving through the entrance, toward their Wing as they always did, when she had slowed then stopped.

"Of course not, I was just inspecting the room, making sure it reflected well on its Lord."

Oryon raised an eyebrow at her words then let his gaze travel around the room. He saw nothing out of place. Warriors gathered here after training or a big hunt, warming themselves before the fire and telling tales. Large chairs and a table were set before the fire for just that reason. House Rigel was not nearly as formal as Torino. It had none of its extravagance or its high shine. House Rigel was a Warrior's House. Did his Isis wish it were something more?

"I see nothing out of place," he told her.

"No, not out of place, just not as well kept as it could be." When Oryon frowned she slipped her arm through his and smiled up at him. "Don't concern yourself. I will speak with Master Kaspar about it later."

"You will do what?" Oryon asked in a deceptively soft voice. Did she really think he would let her 'speak' to Master Kaspar?

"I said," Isis repeated, looking up at him sharply. She knew that tone. It was the one he used when he was extremely 'displeased' with a male, "that I would speak with Master Kaspar about making sure this room was adequately cleaned in the future. There shouldn't be dirt in the corners, and the windows need cleaning."

"You *will not* speak to him," Oryon growled.

"Excuse me?" Isis demanded, jerking her hand from his arm.

"I said..."

"I heard what you said Oryon," she snapped letting all hear she was just as angry as he was. She would not be ordered around as if she were one of his Warriors. She was his 'Lady', and she demanded the same respect from him that he would demand others give her. "I just can't believe you said it. Not to *me*."

With that, she stormed away shocking them all, for none of them had ever heard Lady Isis raise her voice, let alone seen her act this way.

∞ ∞ ∞ ∞ ∞

Oryon watched in confusion as Isis stormed away from him. "Follow her!" he ordered two of his warriors. "See that she makes it to our Wing safely."

"Yes, my Lord." The males bowed and quickly took off after Isis.

"It seems the time spent with the Earth females has Mother forgetting her place." Ull's words had Oryon giving him a sharp look, along with Vali and Zev.

"Her place?" Oryon turned to his first male.

"Yes, she can't just speak to another male. It insults you."

"How does it *insult* me Ull?" Oryon asked softly.

"Her thinking to Join with a male from within your own House." Ull frowned, appearing annoyed that he had to state the obvious.

"And you think that is why your mother wishes to speak to Master Kaspar, to initiate a Joining?" Oryon had to admit that had been his initial kneejerk reaction to Isis' words. It was why he had spoken to her as he had. Now hearing someone else say it, he realized it was absurd.

His Isis loved him, had loved him from the very beginning. She had chosen him twenty-five years ago, and with her every word, every deed, she had proven she'd never regretted it. Not once in all those years had she looked at another male. She had refused all offers. She wasn't going to start now.

She had stated for all to hear *why* she wanted to speak with Master Kaspar. Who was the Master of House Rigel, responsible for making sure the day-to-day operations of the House were taken care of. She wanted more attention paid to the Great Hall's appearance, wanted it to reflect well on *him*. It was something Queen Lisa had done with House Luanda, and obviously, Isis wanted to do the same here.

"Of course. It is the only reason a female speaks to a male," Ull continued.

"So that is what the Empress was doing when she addressed the Assembly? She was looking for a new male to Join with?" Oryon demanded, feeling his anger return. "Is that what Queen Lisa was doing when she also spoke there?"

"No, of course not," Ull said dismissively. "That was different. They are Earth females."

"So you are saying that our Tornian females should be treated differently than Earth females? That they don't have the right to speak to whomever they wish, whenever they wish and not have it mean they are interested in Joining with that male?"

"It's not their way," Ull said.

"It is *my* Lady's way," Oryon growled taking a threatening step toward his first male. He looked to the other males in the room. "And *I* will not have *you* or *anyone* insult *her* by saying otherwise."

Oryon spun on his heel, finding he needed to leave the room before he did something he'd never done before, strike one of his offspring in anger.

∞ ∞ ∞ ∞ ∞

Isis couldn't believe Oryon had spoken to her like that! As if she were some newly Joined female who needed to be told her place. She knew her place and it was no longer being relegated to her chamber. It was at Oryon's side, helping and supporting him with *their* House. At least that's where she wanted it to be. Maybe Oryon didn't feel the same way.

Storming into Oryon's resting chamber, she slammed the door in the faces of the two warriors Oryon had sent after her.

Did he think she didn't know the way? She fumed as she crossed the room. She'd opened the door open to the stairwell that would lead to *her* chambers. Her step faltered. Looking up, she thought about those upper rooms that took up the entire second level of the Lord's Wing.

She had spent over half her life in those rooms, had presented four fit and worthy male offspring there and had watched them grow from its windows. If anyone had asked her before this trip if she were happy in those rooms, she would have said yes.

She couldn't now.

Now she knew there was so much more she could do. So much more she wanted to do. She couldn't go back to those rooms now. They would feel like a prison.

Turning, she glanced around Oryon's resting chamber. She had passed through this room many times in the past, for it was the only way to reach her chamber. An 'extra protection', Tornian females had always been told, so that unfit males could never reach them. Now she wondered if it wasn't just another way to control a female.

She had actually spent very little time in *this* room, with the exception of Joinings. Oryon had always preferred to have their 'discussions' in her rooms, where they wouldn't be interrupted. How strange that seemed to her now, for they could have been 'interrupted' just as easily here during Joinings. Now she wondered if it were so others weren't aware of how much Oryon actually *did* discuss with her.

Was he ashamed of her?

Slowly she walked across the room, taking in the sparsely filled room. The fireplace that had always blazed so brightly, heating the room and allowing her to see her way during their Joinings, was now banked, giving off little warmth. In front of it sat a large couch that upon closer inspection, seemed to have seen better days. Looking around the room, she realized most of the furnishings appeared to be in the same condition. All except for the bed. It was covered in rich fabrics, soft sheets and the pillows she had once said she so loved.

Why had the rest been neglected?

Betelgeuse was a prosperous planet. Why wasn't Oryon using some of that wealth for his own comfort?

Thinking back, she realized most of House Rigel was this way, sparse and... cold... while her rooms never were... Was she to blame for this? Had her staying with Oryon somehow depleted the resources Betelgeuse provided? She had always thought her staying would mean just the opposite, without the need to attract another female, House Rigel would be able to retain more of its wealth. Could she have been wrong?

The sound of the door opening had her turning. Males who served under Master Kaspar, stepped through the threshold, carrying her and Oryon's luggage. When they saw her, they froze, as if shocked at her presence in their Lord's resting chamber.

'Well, they were just going to have to get used to it,' Isis thought because this is where she was staying. "Set them both right there," she ordered pointing to the doors she knew led to Oryon's closet.

"What..." they stuttered, looking at one another in obvious confusion.

"Do as Lady Isis says," Oryon ordered, his deep voice booming as he strode into the chamber, his eyes boring into the males.

"Y... yes my Lord," they said, quickly moving to put the luggage where Isis had indicated before quickly escaping, while their Lord and Lady silently stared at each other.

Oryon slowly approached Isis, trying to assess her mood. She had been so angry when she'd stormed away from him, but now she seemed to have settled, returning to the calm female he'd always known. At least that was the way it appeared.

"You wish to do more than to just rest in my Chamber with me?" he asked tentatively, unsure if that was what having her possessions left here meant.

"Yes," Isis' eyes searching his to see if that upset him. "If you do not mind." She found herself adding.

"Mind..." Oryon reached up to caress her cheek with a knuckle. "There is nothing in the universe that would please me more than to know you were *here* waiting for me."

"I've always been here Oryon," she told him, "but I don't want to just be *waiting* for you anymore, I want to be *a part* of your life."

"You want to speak to whomever you wish." He sighed heavily, rubbing his forehead. "Go wherever you wish inside House Rigel."

"And on the grounds," she told him, her gaze traveling over his suddenly tired-looking face.

"You know that will cause problems," he said, moving away to stand before a window that looked out over the training grounds he had relocated all those years ago so Isis could watch her offspring.

"Why?" she asked coming to stand behind him and placing a gentle hand on his back.

"Because males will think you want to Join with them."

"That's ridiculous." Isis snorted, her eyes looking out to the darkening field. "In all these years I've never considered another male, have refused all offers. I am now forty-three years old and have not presented offspring for over fifteen years. No male would consider Joining with me, even if I offered."

"That is where you are wrong, Isis." Oryon turned to look at her, his hand covering hers. He settled it over his heart. "Any male would be proud to have you as his. Offspring or not. You are beautiful and kind and loving and when they learn about females resting with a male...."

"You are the only male I want to rest with Oryon, the only male I love."

"I know this but... you need to know there are those already wondering, one of them being your own offspring, Ull."

"Ull..." Isis shook her head sadly. "Ull's universe has suddenly shifted and he is no longer sure of his place in it."

"His place? His place is *here*. On Betelgeuse." Oryon frowned down at her.

"Are you sure?" she questioned softly. "I know he always thought it was. There was never any question in his mind that *he* would be the next Lord Rigel. But now his brother... his *third* brother, the one who was supposed to be returning to Betelgeuse to support *him*, to train *his* future warriors and help make *his* House stronger. Now *Ynyr* has been named Lord to a more powerful House than yours."

"None of that stops Ull from one day becoming Lord Rigel," Oryon countered.

"No, it doesn't but as you said, that will be *one* day while *today* Ynyr *is* Lord Rigel. *Today* Ynyr has a female, a female that will most likely give him female offspring. Abby chose Ynyr when she *could* have chosen Ull, just as the Emperor *could* have chosen Ull to rule Etruria. She didn't and he didn't. Now everyone is comparing what Ull will *one day* become to what Ynyr *is*. Ull, for the first time in his life, is being seen as the lesser brother and his pride is stinging." Isis' gaze went to the movement outside on the training field.

"You truly believe this?"

"Don't you?" She pointed out the window to where Ull, in the fading light, had stripped to the waist and was currently pummeling a training station with his sword. Rage filled every movement.

"I've never seen him doubt himself before," Oryon said quietly, watching as large chunks of wood flew from the station.

"He never has. That is why he is struggling so much right now. In time, he will settle and find his way."

"How can you possibly know that?" Oryon turned away from his first male to look at his Lady.

"Because *you* are his manno and you have taught him how to be a truly fit and worthy male. He will find his way, Oryon. His honor will allow him to do no less."

"You are truly a gift from the Goddess, my Isis." Gently he brushed a hand over the top of her head. "One I don't think I have ever treasured enough."

At Oryon's words, Isis felt her eyes fill. She'd always known her male cared for her. It had been in his every touch, every action but to hear him say it…

∞ ∞ ∞ ∞ ∞

"My Lord." Captain Shen stood just inside the doorway of his Lord's resting chamber.

"What is it, Shen?" Oryon asked impatiently, turning to face his long time Captain.

"Your Leads are waiting for you in your Command room." Shen informed his Lord.

Oryon was surprised to find he'd forgotten about the meeting he always had with his Lead Warriors upon his return to Betelgeuse. They would inform him on what had happened in his absence and where his attention needed to be brought to bear first. Oryon found he wanted his attention on his Isis, but he couldn't neglect his duty.

"Tell them I'll be there shortly."

"Yes, my Lord." With a slight bow, Shen turned and left.

"I need to go, Isis."

"But it's getting late, Oryon. Can't it wait until tomorrow?"

"No. I always meet with my Leads when I return. It's necessary, especially this time, when so much has occurred. They will have questions, questions that need to be answered by their Lord so they can then relay correct information to others."

"Information about Bertos and Risa."

"That and about what they need to do if they wish to present themselves to the remaining Earth females. The Emperor's declaration that they may choose any male is going to have every male scrambling."

"Wray also declared that it was now a House's responsibility to make sure the female is well cared for and protected."

"Yes."

"Will House Rigel be able to do that?" she asked hesitantly.

"Of course! Why would you think otherwise?" Oryon frowned at her.

"It's just that the demands extra females make could be a burden on a House."

"And because of that you think I would not be able to adequately provide for *you*?" Oryon couldn't keep the shock or hurt out of his voice. "I have *always* met your *every* need."

"You have and I know you will continue to. That's not what I'm questioning Oryon." Isis tried to calm him quickly.

"Then what *are* you questioning?"

"If House Rigel will have no problem supporting more females, why is its Lord living in a chamber that is as sparsely furnished as the trainees'?"

"What?" Oryon couldn't hide his confusion.

"You are my male, Oryon. My Lord and yet the only comfort you take for yourself is the bed you share with *me*! Why? Has my refusing to leave you put such a burden on our House that you can't even have the most basic of comforts?"

"Isis…" Oryon trailed off when he realized what she was really questioning. She thought their House had suffered because of her, because of what he had given her, when in truth it had flourished. Isis had never made any extravagant demands on him as he had heard other females did. She had certain pillows she liked, would occasionally ask for an expensive fabric but nothing that put a strain on the House's resources. He knew of males who took decades recovering from the demands a female had made on them, while some never did.

"Have I, Oryon?" Isis asked in a wobbly voice.

"No, Isis." He gently pulled her into his arms. "You have not. My chambers are like this because…" He let his gaze travel around the room and shrugged. "I know nothing else. Warriors don't have 'comforts', not like females. My comfort is you. Seeing you. Holding you. Joining with you. It is all I have ever needed."

"But I want you to have more. You deserve more, Oryon. Don't you know that? You are such a good male, so fit and worthy. I know many judged you harshly because of me, because of my refusing to leave you, including the Emperor."

"None of that matters, Isis, because I have *you*. Don't you understand that?" He used his thumbs to wipe the tears from her cheeks.

"They wanted you to force me to leave" she told him and saw his surprise that she knew. "Females do talk Oryon. Not to me, but loud enough to make sure I heard."

"And it never happened. You are *mine*. My Isis, my one comfort. Just the thought of another male touching you that way…" His voice became a deep growl as he spoke. "I'd never allow it. I would kill him first. *You* are *mine*."

"I am," Isis agreed, stretching up to kiss him.

∞ ∞ ∞ ∞ ∞

It was sometime later that Isis angrily eyed the door someone had the nerve to be knocking at. Oryon had left for his meeting and she had been working on bringing things down from 'her' chamber to 'their' chamber. It had started with a rug that she had rolled up and dragged down the curved stairway. It now lay proudly in front of the fire Oryon had made sure was burning brightly before he left.

Next came a small table, which was the only one she could carry. She placed it next to the chair she knew Oryon spent a lot of time in as it had the impression of his body embedded into it. She'd placed an afghan over its back so it would be there when he needed it.

She was just getting ready to tackle their luggage and hang her coverings up next to Oryon's, which she found she really wanted to see, when the knocking had interrupted her.

"What?" She jerked the door open only to find two startled young males from the kitchen staff standing on the other side.

"Lord... Lord Oryon ordered that last meal be... be brought to you, my Lady." One of them stuttered and flushed before he looked away.

Staring at them, Isis suddenly realized they must be new trainees since they appeared years younger than her Zev. It was a common practice to start new trainees in the kitchen to see how they responded to the early morning's pressure and long hours.

Stepping back, she tried to put a serene expression on her face. After all, she *was* their Lady and allowed them to enter the chamber. "Put it over there." She gestured to the low table between the couch and fire.

"Yes my... my Lady," the male stuttered again and they quickly carried the trays in.

"What are your names?" Isis asked.

"My Lady?" The second young male stared at her in shock.

"Your names," she said slowly.

"Umm, I am called Nabil."

"I am Galal," the stutterer said, blushing.

"How long have you been on Betelgeuse?" she asked.

"Two... two weeks," Galal told her.

"I see, well welcome to House Rigel."

"Thank you, my Lady!" they said together.

"Has last meal been delivered to Lord Oryon yet?" she asked.

"No, my Lady," Nabil responded. "Cook said he was not to be disturbed."

"That's ridiculous! It's been hours since midday meal. Give me your comm." She held out her hand.

"I... what, my Lady?" Nabil asked.

"Your comm, I know you have one. All kitchen help does."

"Yes, my Lady." Reaching into his pocket, Nabil pulled out his comm and carefully handed it to her, making sure not to touch her.

Isis took the comm and pressed the only button on it. New trainees were expected to carry it at all times for they were at the disposal of Warrior Lajos, otherwise known as Cook.

"What's taking you little cachus so long?" Lajos angry voice burst out of the comm. "I told you to deliver that food and come straight back!"

"They have delivered my meal, thank you Warrior Lajos," Isis said, her calm voice glaringly opposite of Lajos.

"Lady Isis..." Lajos' tone and volume immediately softened.

"I've been told that last meal has not yet been taken to Lord Oryon and his Leads." Isis got straight to the point.

"No, my Lady," Lajos told her.

"I want it sent now," she ordered.

"I'm sorry but..." Lajos started.

"There are no 'buts' here Warrior Lajos." Isis' voice became as hard and inflexible as any Lord's could be. "Lord Oryon has not eaten since the midday meal on the Hunter. It is now late into the evening. You will send thick sandwiches filled with twrci, rashtar and the queixo made in the Mriga region."

"My Lady," Lajos tried to interrupt.

"I'm not finished. You will also send along an assortment of fruits and drinks. Enough for all the warriors. Is that understood, Lajos?"

"My Lady, you do not understand. Lord Oryon does not like to be interrupted during his meetings with his Leads."

"You are the one who does not understand, Warrior Lajos. I will not have my Lord do without, not anymore. Now you either do as I have ordered or I will come down to the kitchens myself and take care of it."

"I... yes, my Lady," Lajos said suitably chastised.

"And Lajos."

"Yes, my Lady."

"When you deliver the meal, make sure you let your Lord know it was because his Lady ordered you to do so."

"Yes, my Lady."

Ending the call, Isis handed the comm back to Nabil. "Thank you, Nabil. Now you both best hustle back to the kitchen, for I believe Cook will need you."

"Yes, my Lady," they chorused and immediately left.

∞ ∞ ∞ ∞ ∞

"Then there have been no more problems with the training in the Mriga Region?" Oryon asked reading a report.

"No, my Lord. Once the problem with the equipment was discovered and corrected the injuries stopped," one of his Leads informed him.

"And the investigation has been started to find out how the defective equipment got there in the first place?" Oryon asked his voice deceptively soft as he looked to Lead Phong, his Lead in charge of tactics and tracking.

"Yes, my Lord," Lead Phong told him.

Nodding, Oryon relaxed and leaned back in his chair to look at his Captain and Leads. They were good males, every one of them. Most had been with him for years. He wondered which ones would want to go to Luda to see if they could attract an Earth female.

"Now, questions about what occurred on Tornian," he said, because he knew they all had them.

There was silence for several moments before Warrior Eike, Lead for weapons training, spoke. "Is it true that Lord Bertos was attempting to over-throw House Vasteri? That Lord Reeve was assisting him?"

"Yes. Apparently, he and his female had been plotting for years to become Emperor and Empress. Together they were responsible for the attack on King Grim and the deaths of King Rask, Empress Adana and Prince Van. Risa also attacked Empress Kim and tried to kill Princess Destiny. She severely injured the Earth female that was protecting the Princess. The female has made a full recovery," he quickly reassured them knowing they would be concerned, "but Risa was killed during the confrontation by Queen Lisa."

Silence greeted his statement as the Warriors considered what he had said. The loss of a female, any female, meant some male had lost the chance to receive offspring from her. Oryon truly believed that the madness that had affected Risa and her ancestor Emperor Berto would continue to affect any future offspring she produced.

"Then I hope Daco takes them all, for the Goddess would never welcome ones so unworthy," Eike spit out.

Oryon nodded in agreement. "Because of these acts, the Emperor stripped House Reeve and House Bertos of all their power and named two new Lords. Lord Callen of Vesta and Lord Ynyr of Etruria. He also assigned each of us with the task of supporting them while they fix the harm caused, and to build honorable Houses. It is why I left half the warriors with us on Tornian to be split between Lord Callen and Lord Ynyr." Oryon saw his Leads look at each other and ordered, "Speak."

"Why were none of us allowed to assist Ynyr... Lord Ynyr or Lord Callen?" Huntley his youngest Lead asked. It would be a great honor for any warrior to be part of establishing a new house.

"I made that decision and not because I thought any less of those of you here, but because time was of the essence." Oryon's gaze traveled over all his Leads. "Lord Callen left for Vesta three days ago with warriors from the Emperor and every House." Oryon looked at the time unit on his wrist. "They are only now arriving on Vesta. The Emperor charged Prince Tora, who is training on Vesta with controlling the House until Lord Callen arrives. If I were to have sent warriors from Betelgeuse instead of those with me, you would still be two days out because I had our fastest ship on Tornian. It is also why I sent none of you to assist one of our own. After the attack, the Emperor immediately dispatched his own specially trained warriors to Etruria to control Bertos' remaining warriors until he named its new Lord. Ynyr and his Lady arrived in Etruria two days ago."

"Lady!" Every male in the room straightened and leaned a little closer wanting to hear every word.

"Yes, an Earth female named Abby chose Ynyr as her male." Oryon didn't try to keep the pride out of his voice.

"Truly?"

"You did not know this?" Oryon looked at his warriors in surprise. "It happened days ago."

"There were rumors that an Earth female had Joined with a male, my Lord, but we didn't know to whom or if it was even true. We knew the Emperor had dissolved the Joining Ceremony so how could a female Join with a male?" They all looked at Oryon and waited for an explanation.

"That is true. The Emperor *has* done away with the Joining Ceremony. So when Queen Lisa became aware that one of the females under the King's protection wished to Join with a male, they created a new ceremony, one that blended traditions from both worlds. King Grim's 'family' and my family met on the Assembly floor where Abby presented herself to Ynyr."

"Ynyr knew this?"

"No, he did not." Oryon looked at his males and knew he needed to explain further and see if they would react as Ull had. "It seems that Ynyr had... contact with Abby before the Joining Ceremony."

"What!" Every male in the room stood.

"Sit!" Oryon ordered, expecting such a reaction because Abby and Ynyr's actions broke the Law. Slowly his Leads obeyed. "It is not as you think. Ynyr was walking by the walled garden of the female's chamber when he heard a female crying." Oryon saw several of his Leads frown. "He knew it was against the Law for him to approach any of the females before the Ceremony, but he found he couldn't just walk by, and as there was a wall between them...."

"He... spoke to her?" Qays, Oryon's Lead in hand-to-hand training and the quietest of his Leads, asked softly.

"Yes. He was able to calm her. He never told her his name and she never told him hers. They never saw each other, but they spoke through the wall almost daily, telling the other about themselves, about their worlds. It was during this time that Abby developed feelings for him."

"Even though she didn't know who he was? What he could offer?"

"Even though. It seems Earth females must have feelings for a male before they are willing to Join with him... They must have love..." Oryon's use of the ancient word shocked many. "If they do, they will remain with that male."

Stunned silence greeted Oryon.

"She would stay with a male... as Lady Isis has always stayed with you?" Eike asked, the slightest sliver of hope in his voice. "Be *his*?"

Oryon gave Eike a surprised look at what he heard in his voice. He had never considered that one of his Leads, that any other Tornian male might want what he and Isis had. They had always been thought of as the oddity of the universe.

"There is more," Oryon told them. "No longer will a female be forced to choose only from those males that have reached a high status and accumulated enough to support her. From now on she may select *any* that *she* deems fit and worthy."

"But my Lord, how can a male support her if he has no wealth, no status?" Huntley demanded.

"It is now the male's, the female's manno's, and the Lord of the male's House responsibility to make sure she is adequately cared for."

"Their Lord... you would be willing to help us my Lord?" Huntley asked, shock flaring in his eyes.

"Of course!" Oryon looked from Huntley to his other males not understanding why they were so surprised. "You are some of the finest males I have ever had the privilege of knowing. Why would I not be willing to assist you in obtaining a female?"

"But Lady Isis..."

"Is looking forward to having more females on Betelgeuse."

"But... it will take away from what *you* give her."

Before Oryon could respond, a knock sounded on the door. Giving the door an irritated look Oryon, ordered. "Enter!"

Lajos entered, followed by several males carrying platters laden with food.

"What's the meaning of this Lajos?" Oryon demanded.

"Apologies my Lord." Lajos gestured to the males where to put the platters. "I know you prefer not to be disturbed when you are with your Leads, but I was ordered to bring you last meal."

"Ordered? By whom?" Oryon surged from his chair. Only *he* could give that order.

"Lady Isis, my Lord," Lajos told him quietly, his skin darkening in apparent embarrassment as he admitted he had followed a female's order.

"Lady Isis ordered you to bring us a meal?" Oryon sat back down slowly.

"Yes, my Lord. She..." Lajos couldn't keep eye contact with his Lord.

"She what, Lajos?" Oryon asked quietly.

"She threatened to come to the kitchen *herself* and make the meal if her orders weren't followed," Lajos told him, looking sheepish. "I know I shouldn't have...."

"When your Lady gives you an order you will obey it, Warrior Lajos," Oryon told him in a hard voice, "as long as it doesn't endanger her safety."

"Y... yes, my Lord." Lajos gaze flew to the other males who appeared equally shocked.

"Go fill your plates," Oryon ordered his Leads. "Once we have eaten, as my Lady has demanded, I will finish explaining to you more about how our universe has changed.

∞ ∞ ∞ ∞ ∞

Oryon watched as his Leads devoured the food Lajos had brought. Why had he ever insisted they not eat until they were finished? He now realized it might cause his males to rush through the meeting because their hunger distracted them from telling him all they should. How had Isis known this?

"Warriors, our universe has changed drastically since I left for the Joining Ceremony." Oryon watched several Warriors put their plates aside. "Continue to eat, if my Isis discovers you left this meeting hungry she will have my head." He didn't miss the astonished looks on his Warrior's faces.

"You find it strange that I would speak this way to you, when before I left for Tornian, I wouldn't have." Oryon paused, trying to organize his thoughts. "Those of you in this room are among my most trusted Warriors and I consider you as close as brothers." At his statement, every male's chest puffed up. "Many of you, such as Captain Shen, have been at my side since my manno met the Goddess, and I know there have been many trying times. Less worthy males have left House Rigel, choosing to serve elsewhere because they believed my... situation reflected badly on them."

"My Lord," Shen tried to interrupt him, but Oryon waved a hand and Shen snapped his mouth shut.

"It is truth, Shen, and all of you know it. My Isis refused to leave me, even after she presented me with two fit males. Many found fault with me for not forcing her to leave," Oryon let his gazes run over the males in the room. "So she could give her 'gift' to other males, males that could have been you." Oryon's chest tightened at the thought of one of these males he trusted, touching Isis.

"I tell you truth that I would have found myself hard pressed not to kill any male that tried to take my Isis from me *before* going to Tornian. Now, I *will* kill any male that even thinks to take her from me. She is mine!" No male doubted the truth in their Lord's words.

Oryon sighed heavily and tried to calm. "What I need to explain to you is *why* my attitude has changed, and I hope it will explain to you how *your* universe has changed, and that the chance for you to have a female has also changed."

"When Empress Kim was first presented to the Assembly, we all dismissed her as not being a worthy female. Even though she was very similar to our females, she wasn't *really* Tornian, even though the Emperor declared her so.

She was just this small insignificant being to us..." Oryon saw his Leads nod in agreement. "Until she conceived... then we all took notice. We tried to force her to tell us where her planet was so we could acquire more like her, and she refused. She even refused to tell the Emperor. What Tornian female do you know brave enough to refuse her male?" Oryon asked as his eyes traveled over the males in the room.

"My brothers, our females fear us, and it is our fault for we have not given them what they *really* need, and I'm not talking of the 'things' we give them now. The Empress doesn't fear the Emperor because she knows he loves and cares for her as much as she does for him."

"But my Lord," Phong spoke. "They are female."

"Yes, with thoughts, feelings and a mind all their own. That is what we have forgotten with our fear of extinction. Our females aren't *breeders,* as Queen Lisa has accused us of treating them. We aren't like the Ganglians, who just take and use females for their own release. I wish you all could have been there to witness the Queen at the Joining Ceremony, to see not only *how* she stood up to the entire Assembly but how she responded to *anything* she perceived as an insult to King Grim. She defended Grim even though she was attacked while under his protection. She does not view his scars as a sign of weakness but instead as a badge of courage, believing that if he was strong enough to survive that, then he will always be able to protect her and her offspring. It is something *we* should have realized."

Oryon looked to the visual of his manno that still hung on the wall across from his desk. He kept it there to remind him of all his manno had taught him about being a fit and worthy male. Never had Oryon doubted his manno's teachings... Now he did.

"I have never been ashamed to be a Tornian male, until I sat in that Assembly and listened to Queen Lisa. She stood before us, strong and proud and *forced* us to acknowledge that what we had done to them was *no* different than what the Ganglians had done to the Empress. That what *we* had done to our own females made them believe their only value to us *was* as breeders."

"What?" Several males jumped to their feet just as those in the Assembly had, insulted.

"Sit!" Oryon ordered and waited until they did before continuing. "She was not wrong. Is that not why so many looked down on my Isis and her refusal to let herself be used in such a way? In the time since we have left here, I have come to realize that there is the strength of the body that we all hold to such a high standard, and then there is the strength of the spirit that we seem to have forgotten about. Of the two, I have come to believe that it is the strength of spirit that is strongest. It is what enabled the Empress to survive her time with the Ganglians. It was her *spirit*, not her physical strength, which stopped them from breaking her. It is what allowed King Grim to survive his attack when the majority of us would have given up." He paused, looking back to his manno's visual. "What does that say about us as warriors, that we would rather give up, than be judged harshly by others? That the way we *look* matters more than our *actions*?"

"It shames me that we never once considered what abducting those females would mean to *them*. We thought only about our own wants and needs, never theirs. We have done them and our own females a great injustice. Is it any wonder the Goddess has withheld her blessings from us for so long?"

"So we are doomed." Qays said, and Oryon saw the spirit of these fit and worthy males fade.

"No. We are not doomed," Oryon told them. "No thanks to our own deeds and arrogance, but because those same females, the ones we judged so harshly and the ones we thought we could steal without consequence, have shown us the way back into the Goddess' good graces."

"How?" Qays asked.

"By honoring them. By realizing that they truly are the most important thing in all the known universes."

"We already know that." Huntley said.

"That *all* females are," Oryon emphasized. "Tornian or not. They have the *right* to Join with a male... or not. They have the right to choose the male they want, no matter if he's reached a high status or not."

"My Lord, the other females..."

Oryon knew what Phong wanted to ask. "Are under King Grim's protection on Luda."

"So the males on Luda will all have females," Huntley spat out.

"No. I know that is what many are going to think, but the King contacted all the Lords to let them know that it has been decided that for the next two months, *no* male is allowed to present himself to the Earth females, including his own. The females understandably need time to adjust to all we have put them through. In two months, interested males will be allowed to send an *application* to Luda requesting permission to be allowed to present themselves to the females. The *females* will then decide which males are allowed to come to Luda based on that application. Only *then* will a male be allowed to go to Luda."

A stunned silence fell over the room as Oryon finished speaking as each male suddenly realized they *all* had a chance to have a female...

Chapter Three

It was late when Oryon finally returned to his chambers. Much later than he had planned, but once the questions had started, they had just kept coming and he had needed to stay and answer them.

Entering his resting chamber, Oryon found it dark, the only light coming from the dying fire that had once warmed the room. His eyes immediately went to the bed, and finding it empty, felt his heart drop. His Isis wasn't there. Had she become angry that he hadn't returned earlier? It was something he'd never worried about before, her waiting for him.

Crossing the room, he headed up the stairwell. If she was angry, she would just have to get over it for he was never going to rest without her again. Pausing at the top of the stairwell, he was surprised to find a cold darkness greeting him. His Isis never allowed her chambers to become cold and she always left a low light on.

If she wasn't here…

If she wasn't in his bed…

Where was she?

Storming back down the stairs, he was across the room and ready to rouse the entire House when a small movement near the fire caught his eye. Silently, he moved toward it and felt his heart drop again. There she was… his Isis… curled up in his chair covered with an afghan he knew came from her chambers, her head resting against one of the chair's wings, her eyes closed.

There she was. His love.

He must have made a sound because slowly Isis opened her eyes and asked huskily, "Oryon?"

"I'm here Isis," he reassured her, moving to squat down next to the chair, running a gentle hand along her leg. "Why aren't you in bed my love?" The endearment slipped naturally from his lips because it had always been true.

"I was waiting for you," She reached out to caress his cheek. "I didn't want to rest in *our* bed for the first time without you."

Her words had Oryon's heart and eyes filling. *This* was something they should have had for years now. Why hadn't they?

"Oryon?" Isis frowned, seeing his eyes fill. "What's wrong?"

"Nothing is wrong, my Isis. I am just very happy that you are here and I am questioning why it has taken me this long to see that it is where you've always belonged." Isis rewarded his words by leaning forward to capture his lips in a gentle kiss; a kiss Oryon quickly deepened as he lifted her into his arms.

Standing, Oryon carried her to *their* bed.

Isis sighed into Oryon's mouth as he laid her down for the first time in the center of what was *their* bed. This is what she wanted. What she had *always* wanted.

He'd placed her in the center of their bed, her thick black hair spread out around her, the perfect contrast to her pale rosy skin. The love in those dark eyes staring up at him made him feel like the most powerful male in the universe. Sitting back on his heels he let his eyes travel down the beautiful body that had always aroused him. He found she was wearing a covering he'd never seen before. Held up by thin straps, it was silky, with triangles of material that barely covered her breasts.

"What is this?" he asked, running a gentle finger down along the thin strap, caressing the curve of her breast.

"It's a covering I like to rest in," she told him.

"Why have I never seen it before?" he asked gruffly.

"Well," she said, arching up encouraging his finger to continue its journey, "normally when I am here it is to Join, and I am wearing a Joining covering. When you come to my chambers, I wear a robe to cover this because I thought you would not find it appealing."

"You are wrong. I find this very appealing," Oryon told her, leaning down to kiss the valley between her breasts.

"You do?" Isis asked breathlessly.

"Yes, but not as appealing as when you wear nothing at all," he murmured against her skin. Sitting up, he carefully slid the thin straps down, revealing all of her beautiful breasts before continuing to pull until he had completely removed it from her body and tossing it over his shoulder. Now she was naked the way he most loved.

"You are a goddess Isis," he told her his fingers going to his shirt.

"Here, let me help you with that," Isis said, rising to her knees, unconcerned with her nakedness. Her fingers replaced his as she unbuttoned his shirt. Isis took her time with the task, letting her fingers caress each bulge of muscle, and letting them explore each deep crevice that made up his massive chest, before traveling along his toned abs. Her fingers paused at the waist of his pants. Leaning forward, she pressed an open-mouthed kiss to his chest as her hands tugged the shirt loose.

"Isis…" Oryon growled.

"Shhh…" she whispered, "I want to explore you." Dragging her tongue along his chest, she enjoyed his salty flavor, then licked at his nipple, watching it tighten in response. Looking up at him through her lashes, she continued to flick her tongue over it as she asked, "Will you let me?"

"Goddess *yes*," Oryon growled feeling his shaft harden at the sight of her mouth on him. He loved how she licked him as if he were her favorite treat. Shrugging out of his shirt, he let his hands sink into her hair. He wanted to show her just where he wanted her, but she quickly pulled away.

"No," she told him. "Your hands stay here," she ordered softly, pulling them from her hair to press them onto his massive thighs.

At Isis' command, Oryon's eyes widened. He wondered where this bold female was coming from. Never before had his Isis taken control of their Joining, not even in the last weeks when their relationship had changed so drastically. Gripping his thighs, he couldn't help but wonder what she would do next. He didn't have to wait long.

Isis wasn't sure what had caused her to think she could order Oryon around, but when he obeyed, the rush of power she felt was amazing. To have this large, powerful male doing what *she* told him… it made her want to see how far he would let her take it.

Once she was sure Oryon's hands were going to remain where she had placed them, Isis leaned back and let her gaze travel over the magnificent body on display before her. Her Oryon's body rivaled that of a male half his age. He carried no extra weight, as so many other males his age did, Lord and warrior alike. They let their bodies soften as they aged, believing they no longer needed to stay fit. Not her Oryon. He relished his daily workouts with his Warriors and retained all the muscle and strength he'd had when they'd first Joined. It made her want to lick and explore every inch, every crevice. She wanted to try all those things Abby and Kim had told her about.

Would Oryon allow it?

Leaning forward, she gave his other nipple the same attention she'd given its twin, licking and teasing it with her tongue the way Oryon would tease her bud when he pleasured her.

"Goddess Isis." Oryon's entire body jerked, and a tremor ran through him when her mouth latched onto him. His knuckles turned white as he gripped his thighs to prevent himself from throwing her onto the bed and Joining with her. He had told her she could explore him, and he would let her, even if it meant he shamed himself like a young warrior and released in his pants.

Isis couldn't believe that she, a female, was able to make this powerful male tremble and a new sense of confidence surged through Isis, making her bolder. Dragging her nails along his lower abs, she slipped her hands under the waist of Oryon's pants and grazed his shaft, as he sucked in a startled breath.

"Isis!" Oryon's hips surged forward at her touch.

Isis raised her eyes to him and whispered, "I want to see it."

Oryon's hands immediately ripped open the front of his pants, his shaft springing out for her inspection.

"Goddess Oryon…" Isis' eyes widened at the sight before her, in all these years she'd only ever gotten glimpses of this part of him. His shaft was large, larger than she had ever imagined he could be and long, so long. How did that fit inside her? Tentatively, she gripped him and found his skin was hot but so much softer than she'd expected. Squeezing gently, she found the softness ended with his skin, underneath his shaft was as hard as Tornian steel. Slowly, she began to stroke him, finding her fingers couldn't fully encompass him, especially at his even wider base.

As she stroked his shaft, Oryon involuntarily rose on his knees, giving her access, for the first time, to the heavy balls that hung between his legs. The low growl that burst from Oryon's throat as she cupped them had her eyes shooting up to his and she found his own narrowed and glittering.

"Am I hurting you?" she whispered.

"You're killing me," Oryon ground out and immediately saw her pale. She would have jerked her hands away if he hadn't grabbed her wrists. "With pleasure Isis." He ducked his head so she could see the truth in his eyes, then slid her hands back to where they were. "Never has anything felt as amazing as your touch on my body. Don't stop."

"You're sure?" she asked, the bold, confident female disappearing at the thought of causing him pain.

"Yes Isis, touch me."

Slowly, this time much more delicately, Isis let her fingers explore his heavy sacks, gently rolling them in her hands and felt them draw up. Leaving one hand there, she moved the other along his thickening shaft, her thumb gliding along the thick vein on its underside, feeling it pulse.

Reaching the large bulbous head of his shaft, her thumb slowly circled it before gliding along its wide slit, capturing the pearly drops of thick, white fluid that had begun to escape.

Lifting her thumb to her mouth, she closed her eyes as Oryon's strong, sweet and slightly wild flavor exploded across her tongue for the first time. Goddess nothing had ever tasted as good to her. Without conscious thought, she leaned over and gripped his shaft, taking all of him in her mouth.

Oryon's breath left him as he watched his Isis. At first, he had thought nothing could feel better than his Isis' hands exploring his chest, her mouth teasing his nipples. Then she had slipped her hands into his pants, stroking his shaft and that had been better. But she hadn't stopped there; she went on to cradle his balls in her soft hands, causing him to nearly cum then and there, and he knew *that* had been better. *Then*, the seed he had tried so hard to hold back, spilled forth and instead of being offended, she had captured it, tasted it and he knew *nothing* would ever be better than that.

Now, his Isis was doing something he had never even *heard* of a female doing. She was taking him in her mouth and sucking him as if her mouth was her channel. Pumping his shaft in and out of her mouth, she used her tongue to twist and flicker around him.

Goddess! No warrior could be expected to withstand such pleasurable torture.

"Isis!" he roared seconds before grabbing her by the shoulders. Pulling her from his shaft, he ignored her cry of protest, tossed her onto her back in the center of their bed, and covered her.

Isis couldn't believe how amazing this was. She truly hadn't believed Kim and Abby, that it was possible for her to pleasure Oryon with her mouth the same way he did her, and that she would enjoy it.

They had been right. She did. To feel him shake and tremble, and know it was because of what *she* was doing to him was an unbelievable feeling and one she never wanted to end. When he pulled her away from his shaft, she cried out in protest, only to find it cut off as his lips covered hers in a deep, hard kiss, filled with uncontrolled passion.

Feeling his shaft, that had just seconds ago been in her mouth, at her entrance, she eagerly wrapped her arms and legs around him, welcoming him in.

In the back of his mind, Oryon knew he needed to regain his control. He had done nothing to pleasure his Isis. *She* had done all the pleasuring and yet here he was, moments from Joining with her.

"Please Oryon. I need you inside me."

Any possible chance at regaining his control was lost at his Isis' whispered plea and he surged into her with one strong thrust.

"Isis!"

"More Oryon! Goddess more!" She hadn't realized how close she was to her release, hadn't realized that giving Oryon pleasure could bring her pleasure too. She would not forget it in the future, but right now all she could do was feel that sweet, tightening pleasure that would happen just before she released with Oryon deep inside her.

"Oryon!" she cried out in pleasure, her entire body arching up as her release hit her.

Feeling his Isis' body clamping down around him, hearing her cry of pleasure, Oryon thrust one last time, as deeply as he could and roared his release into her.

It was much later, as he was looking down at the sleeping love in his arms that Oryon wondered if he dared confess his years of untruths to her. He had watched her blossom these last few weeks in the presence of the females from Earth. She had found females of like mind and ideals, and it had given her a confidence he had never realized she had lacked.

He had watched her interact with Abby, seen the joy in her eyes at having another female in House Rigel, even if it were just through Joining and not one she presented. What would she do if she discovered he had knowingly prevented her from having more offspring after Zev? That he had denied her the chance to have the female she so desired to have and give him?

Would she still stay with him?

Chapter Four

"Vali will accompany you today when you speak to Master Kaspar," Oryon told Isis as they finished their first meal the next morning in their chambers. Leaning back in his chair, he stared at her and knew he had never seen her look more beautiful than she was at this very moment. She was fresh from his bed, wearing a covering in his House color and the glow from their early morning loving was still on her cheeks.

"Why?" Isis asked, leaning back in her own chair and frowned.

"Because I will not risk a male misunderstanding why you are speaking to him."

"Oryon..." Isis gave him an exasperated look.

"Don't give me that look Isis. I know Queen Lisa travels freely around House Luanda, but she still has Guards that accompany her, and until you do too, either I or one of our offspring will accompany you."

Isis silently looked at him for several minutes then realized he was right. While many things had changed in the last weeks, there were still many risks to being female, mainly because of unfit males. She didn't believe there were any within House Rigel, for Oryon would never tolerate them, but he would still worry, and she wanted to help lighten the burden he carried, not add to it.

"Alright," she told him and smiled as his eyebrows shot up. "You thought I would argue with you."

"I... yes," he admitted.

"Oryon, I am a Tornian female. I know just how dangerous our males can be, especially after what occurred in the Assembly of Lords."

"I will never forgive myself for leaving you unprotected Isis..."

"Stop! I wasn't unprotected. You ordered Zev to stay with me and he did."

"Yes, but..."

"No buts. You did what your honor demanded Oryon. You, Ull, Vali, Ynyr and the rest of our House defended the Emperor. Never have I witnessed such a demonstration of skill, strength and honor against so many unfit males. House Rigel stood tall and proud, showing all that its Lord truly is a fit and worthy male. Even the Emperor was forced to recognize it."

"Emperor Wray has always shown me respect, Isis."

"Perhaps, but not enough and not until *after* you supported him so strongly, and that is because of me."

"Isis..."

"You know it is truth Oryon. The Emperor said as much when he dissolved the Joining Ceremony."

"Perhaps, but I would change *nothing* that has kept you with me Isis, for without you, my life would be meaningless."

Isis gave him a gentle smile. "Nor would I, but our universe *has* changed Oryon. When we left here, I had not one female that I could call a friend. I was forced to watch my offspring grow from afar and was considered an oddity by my own people. Now, not only do I have female friends, but one is the Empress and the other a Queen. I can now openly speak to not only my offspring but to whomever I need. I realize that is going to take time for some to accept, but I am certain your males eventually will."

"Our males, Isis," Oryon told her and she rewarded his words with a brilliant smile.

"Our males," she agreed then frowned. "What else is bothering you?"

"What?" Oryon looked at her in shock. "What do you mean?"

"I don't know. It just seems you are so vehement that you would change nothing. What could you have possibly have changed that you didn't?"

Oryon was saved from answering by Vali knocking on their chamber door.

∞ ∞ ∞ ∞ ∞

Isis smiled up at Vali as he walked beside her through the busy halls of House Rigel. Vali was her second male, barely twenty-four. He wasn't as broadly built as his manno and brothers, but that in no way meant he was weak. She had actually seen Vali outmaneuver Ull in practice, because with that lack of bulk came greater speed and agility. Vali had never bested Ull, but Isis believed that was because Vali refused to do so, fearing others might then question Ull's right to be their Lord.

"How are you handling all these changes, Vali?" she asked.

"What do you mean?" Vali replied, giving a hard look to several males that stared at her a little too long.

"Well, Ynyr is now a Lord. I have yet to hear your opinion on that."

"I will always support my Emperor's decisions," he told her stiffly.

Isis couldn't believe how cold and distant her second male was being. There was a time when she would have allowed it, thinking she had no choice. No longer. Pulling him into a side room, she slammed the door shut before rounding on him.

"What kind of answer is *that*!" she demanded angrily.

"Excuse me?" Vali asked, straightening to his full height.

"Oh no, you won't 'excuse me' in that tone young male. I am your mother, and when I ask you a question, I expect a *real* answer and none of that 'Tornian male' attitude you just gave me. I presented you into this world, and I can take you out of it."

Vali could do nothing but stare at his mother in shock. Who was this female that dared speak to him thusly? Who was standing up to him so fearlessly? He hadn't believed his manno about her keeping her offspring with her for as long as she could. No female did that, but Ull had said he remembered the scent of ardaighs. Vali didn't. Why did he have no memory of that early time with her if it had happened? Had his manno been wrong? Had she had not kept *him* with her as long?

"What is troubling you, Vali?" Isis asked, watching as the dark rims around the outside of Vali's brown eyes thickened ever so slightly, even though his body remained totally relaxed, revealing none of his inner tension.

"Why would you think anything is troubling me?" he asked.

"Because when you are upset your eyes darken. They've done this from the moment you were presented." Isis gave him a small smile as she thought back. "I remember being so worried after your presentation. Your eyes were nearly black, but then you were very upset at being forced into this strange new world. It was only once you were bundled up tight and feeding from my breast that they began to turn the beautiful brown of your manno's."

Vali found himself blushing at his mother's comment. Surely, a mother shouldn't speak of such things to her offspring. Then what she was saying hit him.

"You remember me? Presenting me?" Vali couldn't stop himself from asking.

"Of course I do." Isis frowned at him. "Why would you think I wouldn't?"

"I..." Vali flushed, not sure if he should continue.

"Vali, please... speak freely."

"Manno told us on Tornian that you kept each of us with you for as long as you could before the questions grew too loud."

"Yes I did." Isis nodded in agreement.

"Ull recalled the scent of ardaighs, and whenever he smells them now, it comforts him."

"He did?"

"Yes."

"And this bothers you." Isis could see that it did.

"Yes, because I don't have that memory. Manno said that your rooms have always been filled with ardaighs, so if they are, why don't I remember them?"

"Because you were presented in a different season." Isis could see that Vali didn't understand. "Ardaighs only grow in the gardens during the three months of the warmest season. Ull was presented two months before they bloomed and for some reason we had an extremely long warm season that year. The ardaighs bloomed for over six months. You were presented just as the ardaighs finished their last bloom. That year the cold season never seemed to end and the warm... well I'm not sure we had one. It was then that your manno decided to have a warm season house built. He said he did it so we would always have fresh foodstuffs, but if that were true, then why is so much of it restricted for the sole growing of ardaighs. Your manno did it for me. So I could have them year round."

"Like he moved the training grounds," Vali said.

"He told you about that?" Isis asked, surprised.

"Yes."

"Your manno is such a good male, Vali, but that is not what you are asking, is it? You want to know why you don't have a special memory of me, if your manno thought you would."

"Yes," Vali choked out.

"May I touch you Vali?" Isis asked, stepping closer to him.

"What?" he asked shocked.

"While I know you are my offspring, you are still an adult male and I have no right to touch you without your permission."

"Why do you want to touch me?'

"To show you that while Ull had the scent of my ardaighs, there is something you had that he didn't."

Nodding stiffly Vali braced himself to not feel anything, but the minute he felt his mother's fingers touch his temple, felt the back of them run down his face and jaw, felt them reverse and return their journey, as soon as he felt *that*, he was swamped with the memories of love, of safety, and of *mattering*.

"You were always my most difficult offspring, Vali," Isis said softly. "Not because you were difficult, but because you were my quiet one. You never cried out when you were hungry or when you were wet. You would just look at me with your beautiful, brown eyes and expect me to *know* what you needed. It drove me crazy, until I finally realized that the rim around your eyes would darken when you were upset. After that things became easier."

"No one has ever noticed that before."

"Who have you ever let that close?" Isis asked.

Vali suddenly realized he let no one that close and found his forehead coming to rest on her shoulder as she continued to stroke his cheek.

"Is that all that has been bothering you, my Vali?" Isis asked softly.

"No." And Vali found himself telling her how concerned he was about Ull, about Ynyr, about their Empire.

"What concerns you most about Ull?"

"That he'll never come to terms with being over-shadowed by Ynyr." Vali lifted his head and Isis could see the darkness circling his eyes.

"Is that how he sees it?" Isis asked.

"Yes. First the Emperor chose Ynyr for Etruria and then Abby chose Ynyr because of it."

"That's not why Abby chose Ynyr," Isis corrected him.

"I know this is what has been said, and after meeting Abby I agree, but Ull will never see it that way."

"Because our females always choose the male by his status and what he has accumulated to give her," said Isis.

"Yes."

"Yet Abby chose Ynyr when he literally had nothing to give her, not even a cape."

"That won't last long, for Ynyr is now the Lord of the most prosperous and powerful House in the Empire."

"A House that is in total disarray."

"Truth, but that too won't be for long, not with Ynyr in charge," Vali said confidently.

"You have that much faith in your younger brother." Isis was surprised at the level of admiration she heard in Vali's voice.

"Of course, Ynyr was always meant for more than serving Ull. The only thing holding him back was being..." Vali snapped his mouth shut, as he realized what he was about to say.

"A third male," Isis finished for him. "*My* third offspring."

"I'm sorry Mother. I should not have said that."

"Why? It is truth. I know I have been a great burden not only to this House, but also to my offspring. It was never my intention when I refused to leave your manno that you would suffer for *my* decisions. Perhaps I was wrong."

"No!" Vali instantly denied.

"Vali..."

"You have never caused any of us to suffer and have never been a burden. Yes, others have been critical of our House because you stayed, but their opinions do not matter."

"Even the Emperor's?"

"Especially his, especially now when he has come to realize you had it right all along. *You* held onto your beliefs and honor Mother, when no one else supported you."

"I had your manno," Isis whispered.

"Yes," Vali nodded in agreement, "and the two of you are now showing every Tornian male what he could have... if a female were to choose him, even a Tornian one."

"You make that sound like a bad thing."

"It is." Vali's eyes became thickly rimmed as he looked at her. "Because it is something the majority of us will never have."

"But you *can* have that Vali. You all can."

"There aren't enough females, Mother. Even with the ones from Earth and the new young ones."

Isis felt her heart break for her offspring. "You do not think one would choose you."

"I do not think I have the right to ask. Not when there are others who will need offspring more."

"Others like Ull."

"Yes. He is a first male. He will one day be Lord of Betelgeuse. He *must* have a female for our family line to continue here."

"And your offspring would not do the same thing?"

"They would, but if there can only be one..."

"You would sacrifice for your older brother."

"For my future Lord."

Isis reached out and touched Vali's cheek. "You are a good male Vali, fit and worthy. Your brother is lucky to have you as his second."

Vali felt his cheeks flush at his mother's heartfelt words.

"Together we will all do our best to help Ull see that Ynyr's being chosen as a Lord, and Abby's choosing Ynyr, no way reflects on his fitness as a male or future Lord."

"That may be a difficult task Mother."

"Then let us start now with showing him the beauty of the House that he will one day rule." Slipping her arm through her offspring's, they went in search of Kaspar.

∞ ∞ ∞ ∞ ∞

"You..." Kaspar sat behind the desk in his office and looked at Lady Isis in shock. What was she doing *approaching* him like this? Why was she *speaking* to him? Why was Vali allowing it? "You what?"

"I said I wanted to know why House Rigel's rooms haven't been properly cleaned," Isis repeated herself.

"I personally oversaw the cleaning of your chambers my Lady," Kaspar told her stiffly.

"I wasn't talking about *those* rooms, Master Kaspar. I was referring to the rest of House Rigel. Why are the windows in the entrance hall streaked? Why are the floors dirty? The furniture not properly polished?"

"The entrance is as my Lord desires it," Kaspar responded through gritted teeth.

"You are saying that *my* Lord directed you to leave dirt on the floor? To *not* have the windows cleaned?"

"Of course not!" Kaspar snapped.

"Then why aren't they?" Isis demanded, and Kaspar could do nothing but silently stare at her with blazing eyes. "Gather your males, Master Kaspar," Isis ordered, "and meet me in the entrance hall. There is work to be done, and *I* am going to make sure it's done properly."

"I... you..." Kaspar finally stuttered out unable to believe she thought she could order him around. "You need to return her to her chambers," Kaspar ordered, turning to Vali.

"*Lady* Isis is here with the full approval and support of Lord Oryon, *Master* Kaspar." Vali said in a hard, cold voice, letting the smaller male know just who was in charge here. "*She* is the Lady of this House and *her* orders are to be followed. Unless," Vali raised an eyebrow at Kaspar, "you wish to explain to your Lord why you have disrespected his Lady... and my mother." Vali ended on a growl.

"No! Of course not!" Kaspar instantly denied.

"Then gather your males!" Vali growled.

"Yes, of course, Warrior Vali." Kaspar rose from his desk to leave but Vali's next words stopped him.

"You are leaving without showing your respect for your Lady?"

Turning back, Kaspar found Vali's hand gripping the hilt of his sword and realized the seriousness of his offense. "Pardons," he quickly said, bowing to Vali then shifted to bow to Isis for the first time. "Pardons, my Lady, I will gather my males and meet you in the entrance."

"That will be fine, Master Kaspar." Isis, while gracious at Kaspar's slight, made sure he knew who was in charge. "I'll see you there in ten minutes."

∞ ∞ ∞ ∞ ∞

"Thank you for your support Vali," Isis spoke quietly as they walked toward the entrance hall she wanted cleaned.

"He had no right to disrespect you so." Vali growled his anger at Kaspar's slight. Who did that male think he was? "You are his Lady and my mother!"

"Yes, but it will take time for everyone to adjust to all the changes, not only here but throughout the Empire. There are going to be... misunderstandings."

"That was not a *misunderstanding*. That was Kaspar totally disregarding your position. *You* are Lady Isis of House Rigel. *He* is only the Master of it. He is here to do *your* bidding, *not* question it." Vali looked down at his mother and gave her a slight smile. "I was impressed with how you forgave the slight, and yet you still let him know who was in charge."

"It is something my manno told me many years ago. He told me that when dealing with Tornian males, I would need to speak softly but carry a big stick."

"What?"

The expression on Vali's face had Isis chuckling. "You would need to know my manno to understand." She looked at Vali. "I wish you could have known him."

"He died not long after you Joined with manno, didn't he?"

"Yes, shortly after I presented Ull. There was some sort of accident in his shop. It was never fully explained to me, but he was alone and somehow injured so severely that he died before a Healer could reach him."

"His shop? What kind of shop?" Vali quizzed.

"My manno was a master cabinetmaker." Isis said proudly, then frowned at Vali. "You did not know this?"

"No."

"He loved the feel of adhmad beneath his hands, loved to cut and carve it, to sand and polish a piece until it revealed what it was always meant to be." She paused in the doorway of the entrance hall and looked around the sparsely furnished room. "I have several of his pieces in my chambers. They would fit perfectly here in the hall."

"You wish to bring *female* furniture into the *entrance* hall?" Vali asked in disbelief.

"What's *female* furniture?" Isis asked, trying not to laugh at his aghast expression.

"I... well... small... dainty... fragile... poufy...."

"Is that how you really see females? Even after this last week?" Isis tipped her head to the side, giving him a considering look.

"I... well no, but your furniture..."

"I think you will be pleasantly surprised, and once this room is properly cleaned," Isis glanced around the dirty room they'd entered. "I will show you the pieces your mother's manno made, and then you can tell me if our males will find them comfortable."

As Isis finished speaking, ten males stomped into the room. It was obvious from their annoyed expressions that they weren't happy to be there, and Isis knew exactly who to thank for that, and he was following directly behind them... Kaspar. Well, she wasn't going to let him control her dealings with the males in *her* House. No one would, not any longer.

"Good morning males." Isis stepped forward, letting them know that *she* was in charge here. "I am Lady Isis, as I am sure you are well aware," she smiled at the stunned looks that she was receiving for speaking directly to them. "As I'm sure you've heard by now, drastic changes have occurred in our Empire during the last weeks. Changes such as a female speaking to males she has no wish to Join with." Ignoring their shocked gasps, Isis continued, making sure her eyes met each male. "I do not yet know all your names... but I will." She let that hang there for a moment. "Not, as I have already stated, because I wish to Join with you, but because you are part of *my* House. Part of *my* Lord's House and *he* has chosen you to be here. *He* believes that not only do you belong, but that you are an *asset* to his House."

Her words had the desired affect. Every male straightened their shoulders and puffed out their chests.

Her eyes fastened on Master Kaspar. "Yet this room... it shames the Lord who has shown such faith in you." She saw the shock on every male's face as their eyes frantically traveled around the room.

"Betelgeuse is the 'Hunter's' planet. Our males learn to hunt, track and train here, and become some of the most feared warriors in the universe. That is not an easy thing to accomplish, nor something you can do and remain clean. Yet that does not mean that the place they retreat to after a hunt, the place where they discuss and learn from their 'brothers in arms', must also be filthy. They deserve better than that, and we are going to give it to them."

"You." Isis pointed at a random male. "What is your name?"

"Jael... Jael, my Lady," the young yellow skinned male stuttered.

"It is an honor to meet you, Jael. Now tell me, what do you see when you look around this room?"

"My Lady, I see the entrance hall for House Rigel."

"What else, Jael?" She saw his eyes move to Kaspar. "You are speaking to *me*, Warrior Jael, not Master Kaspar. *I* am asking your opinion."

"I am not a Warrior, Lady Isis," Jael told her, bowing his head in shame.

"You are still in your training?"

"Yes, my Lady."

"How long have you been in House Rigel?"

"Two years, Lady Isis," Jael replied.

"Then I would say you are on your way to proving yourself, Jael, as those found unworthy are quickly weeded out by my Lord. Now tell me if this," she made a sweeping gesture around the room, "was a room that reflected on you personally, what would you change?"

"I, well my Lady, the windows. The dirt on them blocks the light, but if they were clean…"

"It would make the floors look that much worse."

"Yes, my Lady," he said, ducking his head as if he were waiting to be punished for speaking the truth.

"You are correct, Jael."

Isis' words had Jael's eyes shooting to her in shock.

"Jael, I want you and three others to go retrieve ladders so the windows can be cleaned. The rest of you," Isis turned her gaze on the remaining males, "I want you to move this furniture to the side so the floors can be properly cleaned, and that means the entire floor, including every corner. There will be no dirt left in this room."

Silence reigned in the room for several tense seconds before Jael grabbed the arms of the two males next to him, and after giving Isis quick bows, they headed out to get the ladders. Another group went to move the furniture. While several stood next to Kaspar, who hadn't moved.

"Is there a problem, Master Kaspar?" Isis asked, her eyes narrowing on the unmoving males.

"No, my Lady," Kaspar replied.

"Good, so since you forgot to bring the necessary cleaning supplies with you, why don't you and the males at your side go retrieve them. That way they will be available for those that *are* doing as I requested."

"Yes my Lady," Kaspar said through clenched teeth, then giving her only the slightest of bows, spun on his heel, storming from the room quickly followed by three other males.

∞ ∞ ∞ ∞ ∞

Oryon stood hidden in the shadows of the upper corridor that overlooked the entrance hall, his gaze following Kaspar. He had trusted that Vali would see to his mother's safety, but still… he needed to make sure for himself, and the private corridor that led from the Lord's Wing to his command center was the perfect location to observe from. The corridor allowed a Lord quick access to his command center in times of trouble. It also allowed a Lord to see and hear who was in his hall without being observed. Over the years, Oryon had learned a great many things this way, such as Kaspar's barely shown respect for his Lady.

He would have to keep an eye on the male, for while Kaspar had been with House Rigel for many years, he was known to have a short temper and didn't take criticism well, especially not from those he felt were beneath him.

Oryon had tolerated him because he had believed Kaspar ran House Rigel well. Now he would have to rethink that, with Isis pointing out things he had missed. Perhaps it was time for a change.

Seeing Vali look his way, Oryon realized his second male had known he had been there all along. Vali was good that way. He trusted his senses. Turning, Oryon proceeded on to his Command Center, confident Vali had everything under control.

∞ ∞ ∞ ∞ ∞

Kaspar couldn't believe he was following the orders of a *female*.

Lady of House Rigel or not.

He was Warrior Kaspar, Master of House Rigel. *He* had been making sure this House ran efficiently for *years*. That this *female* thought, she had the right to criticize how he carried out his duties was an outrage! She had ordered *him* to fetch the cleaning supplies as if he were a *train...*

Lord Oryon should have gotten rid of her years ago, after she presented him with a second male. For after that, there was no reason to keep her. If he had, Kaspar might have been able to secure a female of his own, but no female would consider him, no matter what he had to offer, because *she* was in this House.

Returning to the hall, Kaspar forced a benign expression on his face, one that he had perfected over the years that masked his inner rage. He knew that the time would come when this female would pay for all the lives she had ruined.

∞ ∞ ∞ ∞ ∞

Isis smiled as her gaze traveled around the entrance hall. The windows now sparkled, letting in so much light that the energy crystals set in bowls along the walls could be conserved for night use only.

Betelgeuse's sunlight revealed every scratch and scar left on its ancient floors by generations of warriors crossing it to warm themselves at the freshly cleaned fireplace. Isis loved every *imperfection*, for it showed this room was used, not just a decoration.

Turning her eyes to the furniture that had been polished to a high shine, she frowned. She moved to the closest chair to inspect it further.

"Master Kaspar!" Isis shouted over her shoulder. "Come here, please." While she added the please, no one doubted it as an order, including Kaspar.

"Yes, my Lady?" The pleasantness in Kaspar's voice sounding forced.

"Why is this furniture in House Rigel?" she demanded, pointing to the array of furniture that had just been cleaned.

"My Lady?" Kaspar gave her a truly confused look.

"This furniture isn't solid adhmad. Why?"

"Of course it is!" Kaspar argued.

"No. It is not!" Isis gave him an angry look. If there was one thing she knew it was adhmad. Her manno had taught her how to recognize all its different varieties in his shop along with what it looked like finished. What she was seeing here was low quality peine covered with a veneer of expensive dair to fool the eye that it was of higher quality. "This," Isis touched the grain of a worn spot on the arm of the chair, "is peine from our southern region. It is not used in furniture such as this, because it is easily damaged. Someone has covered it with a thin layer of dair," she touched the darker grain that had not been worn away, "to make you believe it is solid dair."

"You are wrong," Kaspar argued back. "I personally inspect every piece of furniture made for House Rigel."

"Well, you shouldn't be Master of House Rigel if you are this easily fooled," Isis fired back. "Jael, tip this chair back."

Jael hustled to do his Lady's bidding as the others silently watched.

"Do you see this?" Isis pointed to the underside of one of the chair's legs and the two different types of adhmad were easily seen by all. "Whoever made this left it this way so you would *know* it was not solid dair. If you had 'inspected' this, as you claim you did, then you would have known this wasn't solid dair. I want every piece of furniture in this room tipped." Isis ordered, looking at the other males. "*I* want to inspect each and every piece."

"You are questioning me?" Kaspar couldn't believe it. No one questioned him. "Questioning my abilities!" He took a threatening step towards Isis, who quickly took a step back.

"One more step and I will end you, Kaspar." Vali's low growl had every male in the room freezing.

Master Kaspar's eyes bulged and a thin trickle of blood ran from his neck as Vali pressed his sword against Kaspar's throat.

"Vali," Isis spoke to her second male in a soft, calm voice. "Ease back."

"*No one*," Vali continued to growl, pressing harder against Kaspar's throat, "threatens my mother and lives."

"Vali. Please." Isis tried again, carefully placing a hand on his sword arm. She'd never seen her offspring so enraged. Vali was her calm, steady one, but right now, he was vibrating with rage.

"What in the name of the Goddess is going on?" Oryon demanded, storming into the entrance hall.

Oryon had spent the morning dealing with dozens of decisions that had been left undecided in his absence. Some were important, such as training schedules and the selection of which young males he would be willing to accept for training. Those were decisions that only the Lord could make. Other decisions, he wished he didn't have to perform, such as settling disputes about which farmer they would get their vegetables from this month and which merchant they would give the honor of replacing the House's linens. As midday drew near, he decided it was time to see how things were going in the entrance hall. Finding Vali with his sword at Kaspar's throat wasn't what he had been expecting.

"This *male*," Vali spat out, his eyes never leaving Kaspar, "threatened my mother."

"He *what*?!!" Oryon was quickly at his Isis' side, framing her face with his hands, his eyes searching hers. "Isis?"

"I am fine," Isis told him, putting a reassuring hand over his.

"What happened?" Oryon demanded.

"Master Kaspar became... upset when I questioned his ability to distinguish quality furniture from inferior."

"Furniture?" Oryon's eyes flew to all the tipped furniture in the room.

"Yes," Isis told him.

"You do not believe these are worthy pieces to be in House Rigel?" he asked, then looked to Vali. "Lower your sword, Vali." When Vali didn't immediately do as he had ordered, Oryon growled at him. "*Now Vali*! I want to hear Master Kaspar's response."

Slowly Vali lowered his sword, but he did not sheath it.

"You questioned my Lady's ability in judging furniture, Master Kaspar?" Oryon asked in a deceptively calm voice.

"Sire," Kaspar croaked out, his hand going to his injured throat. "I was merely trying to explain to your Lady that she was mistaken. I was only moving toward her to point out why. Warrior Vali overreacted to my move."

"Really?" Oryon eyed his offspring, knowing Vali *never* overreacted. If he sensed a threat, there was one.

"Yes, my Lord," Kaspar said.

"You question my Lady's knowledge of furniture?"

"My Lord, I know I shouldn't have, because of her position, but when she was so obviously wrong, I felt it was necessary to correct her. It is understandable of course, I mean, she is female."

Oryon silently stared at Kaspar before speaking. "Did you know, Master Kaspar, that my Isis' manno was the Master Cabinetmaker for House Torino?"

"I..." Kaspar's gaze flew to Isis, and he found her staring back at him, standing tall and proud. "No, my Lord, I didn't."

"He was a rare male, was Master Geb. He believed that his female offspring should be knowledgeable and educated. He taught her many things. One of those things was his own craft, that of working with adhmad." Oryon let his words hang there before turning back to Isis. "Show me what you have discovered, my Lady."

Isis looked at Oryon for a moment then turned to the piece in question. "This chair is made from peine, a low quality, soft wood that's been covered with a thin layer of dair." She pointed to the different woods as she spoke. "I don't believe the maker of this ever intended for someone to believe it was solid dair. If he had, he would have put a thick piece of dair on the base of every leg so no one inspecting it would know."

"Yet there isn't," Oryon said.

"No, there isn't."

"The other pieces?" Oryon let his gaze travel around the room.

"I haven't inspected them yet."

"Please do so, Isis, I need to know what we are dealing with."

Nodding, Isis turned and carefully began to inspect each piece that filled the entrance hall of House Rigel. She felt her anger grow. Every piece in this room was the same as the chair... substandard furniture. Why?

Oryon crossed his arms over his chest and silently stared at Kaspar as Isis inspected the furniture.

"My Lord," Kaspar began.

"Silence!" Oryon ordered. "We will wait to hear what my Lady discovers."

"But my Lord!"

"Do you want to meet *my* sword, Kaspar?" Oryon growled gripping the hilt of his sword. "Because I promise you, I will draw more blood than that pitiful trickle that my male did."

At Oryon's words, Kaspar stiffened, knowing that when Lord Oryon drew his sword he would strike true and Kaspar wasn't ready to meet the Goddess this day.

Seeing Isis approach, Oryon turned his back on Kaspar.

"What did you discover, my Isis?" Oryon asked in a strong but gentle voice.

"It is all the same, peine covered with dair, but I also found a craftsman's mark."

"Who?"

"A Master Bard."

"Bard?"

"Yes. You know him?"

"He is my Master Cabinetmaker. Kaspar?" Oryon's eyes pinned the male he had trusted to run his House.

"Sire, I have no knowledge of how this could have happened."

"Are you not the Master of House Rigel?" Oryon demanded.

"Yes, my Lord."

"Are you not in charge of running and obtaining the furnishings for this House?"

"Yes, my Lord."

"Yet you claim no knowledge of this."

"No, my Lord... I mean yes, my Lord," Kaspar stumbled over his words. "I have no knowledge."

"Gather your accounts, Master Kaspar, and meet me in my command center in twenty minutes."

"Yes, my Lord." Spinning around on his heel, Kaspar all but ran from the hall.

"Get this crap out of my House!" Oryon ordered the remaining males, who quickly rushed to do their Lord's bidding. "Vali, escort your mother back to our chambers and remain with her."

"Yes, Manno."

"Oryon." Isis put a gentle hand on his arm, frowning.

"I want to know where you are and that you are safe while I sort this out Isis. Something isn't right."

Isis wasn't sure what Oryon was sensing, but she trusted him. "Alright, but may we take several of the trainees with us? We can use this time to sort through the furniture in my old chambers and have the appropriate pieces sent down for the entrance until replacements can be made."

"Isis..." Oryon couldn't believe what she was saying.

"I think my manno would be extremely honored to have what he built used in *your* entrance hall." She looked around the room. "He used to tell me stories about the hunts he had here as a young warrior." Moving, she allowed her hand to caress the silky texture of the mantle, knowing her manno had done this exact same thing sometime in the past. "How he loved to sit in front of this fireplace with the Emperor's manno, before he was Emperor, and tell their stories..."

Isis, lost in her memories, was unaware of the effect her words had on the other males in the room.

"The honor is mine, Isis," Oryon told her quietly. "For your manno was a truly fit, worthy and a talented male."

"He was." Isis felt her eyes fill with tears as she remembered her manno, remembered all he had given her, and it was so much more than furniture. He was the one who had told her she had the right to stay with just one male, if that was what she wished. He told her that he would support that decision, no matter the offspring she presented, if her male made her happy.

Isis' own mother, Nurit, had wanted to stay with him, but when she had presented Isis, the pressure from Nurit's manno and the promises of what other males would offer for sharing her 'gift' with them, had become too great and she had left. Isis didn't think her manno had ever truly recovered.

Years later, when her mother came to help Isis present Ull, Isis discovered her mother had always regretted that decision. It had changed her; she was no longer the gentle female her manno had always told her about; she had become a spiteful and bitter female who after each offspring Isis presented, had encouraged her to leave Oryon. By the time Isis had conceived Zev, she had refused to allow Oryon to contact her, preferring to stay alone and have a Healer assist her.

It had been a difficult time and her presentation had not gone well. It is why Isis believed she had never been able to conceive again, even though she was still young enough too. It hadn't mattered to Oryon, but she'd always wanted to give him a female.

"Isis..." Oryon reached out, cupping her cheek, when he saw her eyes cloud over and fill. He knew she had been close to her manno, closer than any female normally was and that she still mourned him. It was a tribute to the male Geb had been. Oryon wished he could say the same about her mother.

Nurit had been a conniving female and it still amazed Oryon that she could have produced such a wonderful female as his Isis. Every time he called her to assist Isis in her presentation, Nurit had demanded more and more tribute, not caring that Isis would suffer without her. She hadn't liked that Oryon had visited Isis after she had conceived, stating it was inappropriate. Oryon couldn't have cared less what Nurit thought. Isis was *his* female. She carried *his* offspring. It was what *Isis* thought that mattered and she wanted to see him.

"I'm sorry, I let my mind wander." Tipping her head into his hand, Isis gave him a small smile.

"About your manno."

"Yes, you know me well."

"I do my Isis." He let his fingers caress her cheek.

The sound of a bell ringing, announcing that the midday meal was ready, had both of them remembering where they were.

"If you agree, I'll have Jael and those who helped him with the ladders come to our Wing after midday meal and carry furniture."

Oryon looked at Jael as the other three stepped next to him. He recognized these trainees and they were satisfactory. "They will be fine. I'll have Lajos send up a meal for you and Vali."

"What about you?" Isis asked. "You need to eat too."

"I will, *after* I deal with Kaspar."

"Alright." Isis nodded. "I will see you later." Turning, she nodded to Vali and they left the hall.

∞ ∞ ∞ ∞ ∞

Oryon waited until Isis was out of earshot before speaking. His gaze traveled over each male assessing him as his stare kept them in place. "I want you to speak now if you have any knowledge about what occurred here today. If I find out later that you do and did not speak you will be dealt with harshly by *me*."

Absolute silence greeted Oryon's statement. Every male knew he would force the offending male or males out of his House in disgrace if he discovered they were lying to him.

"Jael." Oryon turned hard eyes on the young male when no one spoke.

A slight tremor swept visibly over him. "Y...Yes my Lord."

"You, Fajr, Abir, and Eben will eat first then immediately proceed to my Lady's chambers where you will do as she commands. Is that understood?"

"Yes, my Lord," they said as one.

"Then what are you doing standing here!" Oryon roared. "Go! Eat! All of you!"

At his words, they stampeded out as one.

Chapter Five

At what he was seeing, Vali's eyes widened in shock. He had heard tales of what a female's chamber would look like and how they were filled with luxerious treasures from every known universes. It was why males worked so hard, so they could amass the items they would need to fill such rooms, but this, this was something he could never have imagined.

"You seem surprised Vali," Isis said quietly.

"I... well... yes."

"Why?" Isis asked, looking around her rooms.

"Because, it is not how I always imagined it would be."

"It isn't? How did you imagine it?'

"I don't know. Fuller... Lusher... Overflowing." His eyes continued to travel around the room. Yes, the room contained rich fabrics that a male's rooms would never have, but they weren't in the abundance he'd been led to expect. Yes, there was furniture, but it wasn't the dainty pieces he'd been told female's preferred, but sturdy pieces that would comfortably hold a Tornian warrior. His eyes zeroed in on a specific piece, sitting next to a window.

Isis walked over to the chair her offspring's eyes seemed focused on, "Do you like it?" she asked, running her hand lovingly along the smooth wood of its high back.

"It is an extraordinary piece," Vali said, knowing he had never seen anything like it. The chair was an unusual size, not quite large enough to fit the form of a Tornian male the size of his manno, but not the size of his mother either. Its material wasn't the rich 'female' fabric either. Instead, it was covered in well-worn liedr, the skin of one of their most feared animals. It was something he never expected to find in her room. Why was it here?

"Come. Sit." Isis encouraged him.

"No! I couldn't," he told her.

"Why not?" Isis asked, seeing the desire in his eyes. "This was my manno's favorite chair. He designed it specifically for his height and build. Please?" she asked softly. "I would very much like to see you in it."

Walking over Vali slowly lowered himself into the chair, then leaned back to find it fit him perfectly. Running his hands along the arms, he found the liedr soft and supple, telling him it was well cared for and often used. Next to the chair was a table that could only have been made specifically for this chair, as it was the perfect height. On the table, a book lay open, face down. Looking out the window the chair faced, he discovered he had the perfect view of the practice fields below. His manno had been right about her watching them. Lifting his eyes, he found his mother watching him with the strangest look in her eye.

"You look so like my manno sitting there," she said quietly. "I never realized that before because you are also so like *your* manno."

"Your manno truly made this?" he asked, his eyes returning to the chair.

"Yes. It and the table were the only pieces he ever made specifically for himself. He would sit in that chair and design his next piece or he would hold me when I had a nightmare and tell me he loved me." Tears filled Isis' eyes as she spoke.

"I wish I could have known him," Vali told her.

"So do I."

Before Vali could speak again, his comm rang. "Yes?"

"Warrior Vali there are four males here saying they are to report to you," one of the guards at the Wing's doors informed him.

"Yes, send them up." Vali rose from the chair. "Are you sure you want to move these pieces to the Entrance Hall?" Vali let his eyes travel around the room again, this time easily picking out the pieces his mother's manno had made.

"Yes, our males need places to sit after a long, hard day. My manno's pieces were designed specifically for that."

"But the fabric..."

"Is more durable than you think, and if it is damaged, it can easily be recovered. Don't worry so."

"But if we take these pieces the majority of this room will be empty."

"Which is fine, since I'm no longer staying in these rooms."

"You're not?!!" Vali's eyes went wide.

"No. I am now staying in the Lord's Chambers," Isis told him with great satisfaction. "It's where I should have been all along."

"I..." Before Vali could say more, the sound of hesitant footsteps on the stairs stopped him. Moving to place himself between the stairs and his mother, he put his hand on the hilt of his sword, removing it only after he verified that it was only the four males his manno had sent.

"Hello, Jael," Isis smiled as she moved around Vali. "And who have you brought with you?"

"This is Abir, Fajr, and Eben, my Lady." Each male bowed to her as Jael introduced them.

"You are all in your second year of training?" Isis asked.

"Yes, my Lady," they told her.

"Then soon it will be *you* that will be resting on this furniture before your Lord's entrance fire."

Vali had to hide his smile as the chests of all four males puffed up at his mother's words. They knew only those in their final years of warrior training were allowed to sit in the entrance hall. For their Lady to say such a thing meant she believed in them.

"Now," Isis continued, "I want everything in this room, with the exception of the chair and table by the window, and the things I place on the mantle, taken to the entrance hall, starting with this couch." She touched the piece she was referring too. "It will take all four of you to carry it, for it is solid dair and very heavy. Take your time with it, and if you find you need extra help, make sure you get it. I don't want you hurt. You matter more than any piece of furniture." Picking up several items, she turned and went to put them on the mantle.

Isis didn't see the shocked looks on the trainees' faces, but Vali did. He knew that with those simple words of caring, his mother had secured the loyalty of these four and she hadn't even meant too.

"Yes, my Lady," they quickly said and immediately did her bidding.

∞ ∞ ∞ ∞ ∞

Oryon took his time studying the order slips before him. They were hand written by Master Kaspar, stating in exacting detail what was to be made for House Rigel, maybe too exacting. There were two signatures on each invoice. Master Kaspar's and Master Bard's, along with what Master Bard was compensated.

"As you can see my Lord, it is as I have said. Solid dair furniture was ordered."

"Yet that's not what was received," Oryon stated, leaning back in his chair.

"If that is truth, I was unaware of it until today."

"If?" Oryon growled at Kaspar.

"My Lord, while I understand you supporting your Lady before the trainees, it is not necessary to do so before me."

"You believe I would speak an untruth... before my males... because my Lady was present?" Oryon's voice grew with each word.

"Only to not upset your female. I know she *believes* she is correct."

"Did you not listen to my words about who my *Lady's* manno was?" Oryon stressed Isis' title.

"Of course, my Lord, but it's not as if Master Geb would have *actually* taught her anything." Kaspar's words indicated that the very thought was ridiculous to him.

"So you doubt *my* words." Oryon's tone became lethal.

Kaspar's gaze flew over his Lord's face. He finally realized that his Lord had not just been humoring his female. He actually *believed* her about the furniture. *Her*, a *female*, before *him*, a trusted high-ranking *male* in his House.

"I... my Lord... I would never..."

"Yet you just did, Master Kaspar! *I* say that the furniture is inferior and *not* solid dair as these invoices say! *Why?!!*"

"I... my Lord... I do not know!"

"I want *all* the invoices for this House brought to me! Every. Single. One. Do you understand Kaspar?"

"I... yes, my Lord. It will take me a little time to gather them."

"You have three hours Master Kaspar and then I want you back here."

"Yes, my Lord."

"While you are doing that I will get to the bottom of the furniture with Master Bard."

Kaspar paled at his Lord's words. "I... yes my Lord... three hours." Spinning on his heel, Kaspar quickly left the room, his mind racing. If Oryon talked to Bard, he would discover Kaspar's deception. What was he going to do? As he rushed around the corner, he plowed into Jago.

"Hey!" Jago grunted, shoving Kaspar away. "Watch where you're going!" Jago had never liked Kaspar, even before he had become Master of House Rigel. Although they were the same age, Kaspar had been several years ahead of Jago in his training, due to Jago's problems on Luda, and Kaspar had never let him forget it. Not that Kaspar had known the reason... no one had except Lord Oryon, and he had kept that to himself. It was something Jago had been grateful for, but now, because of what happened on Tornian, everyone knew, and he was being treated differently. It was why he was on his way to speak to his Lord.

"You watch where *you're* going! You drunkard!" Kaspar spat at him, telling Jago word had spread throughout Betelgeuse of his shameful past. Shoving Jago aside, Kaspar continued on his way.

∞ ∞ ∞ ∞ ∞

Oryon was gathering the invoices Kaspar had left and was rising to leave when there was a knock on his door.

"Enter!" he commanded and was surprised to find Jago entering.

"My Lord." Jago's arm crossed his chest, as he bowed to the male that had given him back his honor.

"Jago, what can I do for you?" Oryon sank back in his chair.

"My Lord, before you stands a male that only exists because of you. You allowed me to recover my honor and rise above my past. I repaid that by bringing shame onto your House."

"Jago..." Oryon was shocked by the young male's statement and was about to tell him so, but Jago continued.

"I need to request that you release me from my vow to you."

"Why?" Oryon demanded.

"Because I don't want to bring more dishonor to your House."

"Where would you go?"

"I... I don't know yet but..."

"No." When Jago opened his mouth to argue, Oryon ordered, "Sit!"

Slowly Jago did as his Lord ordered.

"Now tell me exactly what's going on."

"My Lord, I told you."

"This is because of what was made known on Tornian."

"Yes, my Lord," Jago told him quietly. "I can no longer serve..."

"Why?" Oryon demanded. "What has changed?"

"My Lord?" Jago gave him a stunned look.

"What has changed, Jago? Except the fact that everyone now knows what you have had to overcome to become the fit and honorable male you now are."

"My Lord?" Surprise flared in Jago's eyes.

"It took a male of great honor and courage to do what you did in front of the Assembly, Jago. In front of the Emperor. You stood and told truth, even though it reflected badly on the male *you had been*. You showed that a male, a Tornian male *can* change, that who we *can be* is not dictated by who we *were*. I am proud that you are a member of my House."

"But others..."

"*That's* what this is about? What others are thinking and saying? Jago, you can't let that control you. If I had, I would not have four males that I am extremely proud of. I wouldn't have my Lady, who I would give my life for and not because of the offspring she has given me, but because she completes me in a way I can never truly explain. Without her, you may as well end me."

Shock widening his eyes, Jago sat back in his chair. "Your Lady is an extremely special female my Lord."

"She is, and right now she is in her old chambers selecting furniture for the entrance hall. This conversation is done. You will stay as you vowed. You are an asset to my House, Warrior Jago, not a liability, and I mean to keep you."

"Thank you, my Lord." Starting to rise, Jago paused. "My Lord?"

"Yes?" Oryon stood, gathering the invoices.

"Why is Lady Isis selecting furniture for the entrance hall?"

"Because it seems Master Bard has been passing off inferior furniture as solid dair."

"Impossible!" Jago immediately denied the possibility.

"Excuse me?" Oryon asked, raising an eyebrow.

"Master Bard would never do such a thing, my Lord. He is a fit and honorable male who takes great pride in his work."

"Yet I have invoices in my hand." Oryon lifted them. "Signed by him that state he made solid dair furniture for my hall, when what was found is peine covered with dair."

"All I know is that if that is what you have, then that is what Master Bard was requested to build."

"You have that much faith in the male?"

"Yes, my Lord." Jago simply said.

"Then you will accompany me while I confront him with this, and we'll see if your faith is well placed."

"Gladly, my Lord."

$$\infty \ \infty \ \infty \ \infty \ \infty$$

Master Bard's shop was several maili from House Rigel in a small valley surrounded by a heavily forested area. Bard would sometimes work late into the night and the landscape kept the noise from traveling, as it was doing now.

Oryon knew Bard was well liked by his people, not only because he was an outgoing male, but also because he was very talented. His furniture was highly sought after. It was why Oryon had made him his Master Cabinetmaker, securing that House Rigel would always have the best. Or so he had thought. Now he wondered if he had been made a fool of.

"Master Bard!" Oryon roared over the noise of the saw, as he entered Bard's workshop.

After several moments, Bard shut off his saw. "Who in the name of the Goddess would *dare* roar at a male when he is using the saw?!!!" Bard spun around, little pieces of adhmad clinging to his gray hair, revealing his advanced age. He didn't appear fazed at seeing Oryon. "Did you *want* me to cut off an arm! My Lord," he tacked on at the end.

Oryon held back a smirk at the older male barely remembered show of respect. It was something he had always liked about the male. He saw Oryon as just another young male, one that *he* had something to teach. The thought that he had fooled him for all these years had Oryon frowning.

"I am here to speak to you about the furnishings in the entrance hall of House Rigel."

"What about them?" Bard snorted, turning back to inspect the piece of adhmad he'd been working on before he'd been interrupted. "Still can't believe you ordered it. If having a Lady has put that much of a strain on your Household, then you need to get rid of her. House Rigel's entrance hall, hell the whole House should only have the best Betelgeuse has to offer, not pieces that only *look* it."

"What?" Oryon asked in a deadly quiet voice.

"Have you gone deaf, my Lord? Or is it that you just don't like to hear truth anymore?" It seemed Bard was years past caring if his Lord ended him.

"I am not deaf and I will always listen to truth, old male, and you better start giving me some. I want to know why the furniture in my hall is not what was ordered!"

"It was *exactly* what was ordered, although it pained me to make it!"

"I have the invoices right *here*!" Oryon shouted, pulling them out of his inner pocket. "Furnishings made of *solid dair* were ordered!"

"It was not!" Bard shouted back.

Moving forward, Bard grabbed the papers from Oryon's hand faster than Oryon thought he could, for the male had a limp, an injury Bard sustained in a battle that had nearly cost him his life. It was why he no longer carried 'Warrior' status.

"What is this?" Bard scanned the pages.

"It's the invoices for the entrance hall furniture you made."

"That's an untruth!" Spinning around on his good leg, Bard limped toward his office, muttering the entire way.

Oryon raised an eyebrow at Jago, who just shrugged, and they both followed the older male. When they reached the little room that seemed to be Bard's office, they found him still muttering about incompetent young males as he opened and closed file drawers.

Looking around the room, Oryon found it surprisingly clean and organized. Walking over to a tall, design desk, he found what would be an amazing piece of furniture still being designed. It was large and solid, yet had the beautiful carving and detail work Oryon knew Isis so loved.

"Here!" Bard exclaimed triumphantly.

The slamming of a file down on anther desk had Oryon turning around to find Bard flipping through papers. Pulling one out, Bard shoved it into his Lord's hands. Looking down, Oryon saw that it appeared to be an identical invoice to what Oryon had given him, only this one stated peine covered with dair and an entirely different price. One that was a great deal lower then what Kaspar stated he paid.

Sliding Bard's invoice on top of the one Kaspar gave him, Oryon discovered the signatures lined up perfectly as did the invoice numbers. It was only the descriptions and amounts, which were different. Oryon felt his rage begin to grow, but knew he had to suppress it.

Bard felt no such inclination. "That son of Daco! I knew I should have come to Rigel and spoken of my disgust straight to you!" Spinning on his bad leg, Bard, had to catch himself as his knee gave out. He flushed as if embarrassed by his show of weakness.

"Why didn't you?" Oryon demanded, but not as vehemently as he would have seeing Bard's stumble.

"Because that Daco dung House Master of yours, Kaspar, informed me that he had also tried to get you to change the order, and you informed him that *you* were Lord of House Rigel and if anyone else questioned his decisions they would find them off Betelgeuse." Bard's flush darkened and he whispered so quietly that Oryon barley heard him. "I have nowhere else to go."

Oryon felt his stomach clench at this proud male's words. That one so proud could believe he was valued so little by his Lord should never have happened.

"I would never have done that Master Bard." Oryon walked over and squeezed Bard's shoulder reassuringly. "You have served not only my manno but myself loyally and well. We don't toss aside those that do that. You will always have a place in House Rigel."

"Thank you, my Lord." This time Bard's voice held only honest respect for his Lord.

Nodding, knowing Bard was uncomfortable, Oryon got back to the subject at hand. "When did Kaspar tell you this?"

"It's been over five years now, my Lord. Starting with the tables for the eating hall."

Oryon frowned at this, remembering how the legs of several tables had broken, injuring several trainees. Kaspar had told him the trainees had been rough housing, causing the tables to break. Now he wondered.

"You have an invoice for every piece made?"

"Yes, my Lord. I will get them for you."

"No need, Master Bard." Oryon stopped him. "Your word is good enough for me. I want you to remake each piece as it *should* have been made. I will only have *quality* in my House."

"Yes, my Lord." Bard bowed to him. "My Lord..."

The hesitation in Bard's voice had Oryon giving him a hard look.

"What Master Bard?"

"The other furnishings?"

"Will be destroyed."

"I..."

"What Master Bard?"

"My Lord, there are those that could use those pieces, those that are unable to purchase solid dair."

"You will remove the House Rigel emblem from them?" Oryon wanted no one thinking it was something that his House claimed.

"Of course, my Lord."

"Then I will have them sent to you... *after* I see to Master Kaspar."

"Deal with him harshly my Lord," Bard said, "and check all the invoices. If he has done this to me, then he will have done it to others."

"I will. Have no doubt of that. Kaspar has sealed his fate with his dishonor."

Chapter Six

Kaspar stood frozen, looking around his office, trying to decide what to do. There was no way he could get to Bard's invoices and change them. That unfit male kept immaculate records. When Lord Oryon discovered his deception... even if Kaspar was able to shift the blame to someone else, Oryon would still blame him for not inspecting the furniture, and then there was the difference in costs. *That* only Kaspar could have done.

Realizing this was all going to come back on him, Kaspar began to sweat. He needed to destroy the evidence of his crimes, needed time to get away before they were discovered. He frantically looked around the room. He needed a distraction.

Moving toward a hidden compartment in the wall, he quickly opened it, pulling out the heavy bag of credits he had been able to acquire over the last five years. Shoving them into another bag, he dropped it near the door, then turned back and began emptying his files, piling everything in the center of his desk. Grabbing a glowing stick from the fire, he threw it onto the pile. At the door, he snatched up the bag of credits and waited long enough to make sure the papers caught, then left the room, closing the door to his crimes behind him.

∞ ∞ ∞ ∞ ∞

"Right there, Jael." Isis pointed to the spot in front of the fireplace where she wanted the couch. They had finally emptied nearly her entire first room, so she and Vali were now in the entrance hall, seeing to the placement of the pieces. Her father's couch was going to take pride and center in Oryon's entrance hall. Seeing it there, Isis felt her eyes fill, she couldn't believe it had taken her this long to realize that *this* was where it was always meant to be, just as she was meant to be in Oryon's chamber.

"It looks like it was specifically made for that spot mother." Vali came up behind her, putting a gentle hand on her back.

"It does," she whispered. "He would be so honored to have it here, knowing it was going to be used not only by the warriors of House Rigel, but by *my* males."

"We will treat it with the respect it deserves."

Isis smiled at that. "You will use it as it was meant to be used, as a comfortable place to relax and, when its usefulness is done, another will replace it."

"There are certain things that can never be replaced, mother," Vali told her softly.

"Things can always be replaced. People can not, Vali."

"My Lady," Jael stepped up to her. "Where would you like the remaining pieces?"

The remainder of the afternoon seemed to fly by as House Rigel's entrance hall was transformed into a place where every warrior was going to want to relax. Looking around the room, Vali couldn't believe the difference. Just yesterday, when he had passed through this hall he hadn't wanted to stop, preferring his own chambers. Now, he knew he would want to spend time here. There were thick rugs covering the cool stone floors, light was streaming in through sparkling windows, and the room had a warmth that had nothing to do with the roaring fire. It came from the care and thought his mother had put into the placement of every piece, seeming to know what a male would want after a hard day of training. He had never thought a 'female's' touch could make such a difference.

"Jael, I know it is getting late, but there are two more pieces from my room that I would like moved. A chair and a table."

"Of course, my Lady," Jael replied. "Where would you like them placed?"

"Mother..." Vali knew that she was referring to the pieces in front of the window, her father's custom pieces. "Those need to stay with you."

Ignoring him, Isis continued to talk to Jael. "You will need to ask Vali that question, as you will be taking them to his chambers."

"What?" Vali gave his mother a shocked look. Why would she give *him* pieces that were so dear to *her*?

"Of all my offspring, Vali," Isis gave him a soft look, "*you* are the most like my manno. You have the heart of a warrior and the sensitive soul of the Goddess. That is a gift, not a weakness, as some would think, for it allows you to see what others miss. You, above all others, will appreciate what my manno created and the skill it took to do so, and when *you* have offspring, you will be able to sit there and tell them about your mother's manno."

"You truly honor me Mother." Vali's voice strained with emotion as he crossed his hand across his chest, giving her a deep bow, showing her the greatest respect a Tornian male could to a female he wasn't Joined with.

"It has always been *my* honor to have you and your brothers for offspring. It was one of the reasons the Goddess created me."

"And the other?" Vali found himself asking as he rose, and his mother smiled at him.

"To love your manno, of course. *He* is my destiny."

∞ ∞ ∞ ∞ ∞

"Jago, when we get back to Rigel I want you to gather a dozen warriors, your most trusted."

Oryon's words caught Jago by surprise as they strode back to House Rigel. "My Lord?" he asked.

"You have more than proven yourself to me, and I trust your sense of honor." Oryon's eyes shot to him. "Your inner strength is impressive. We all have things we are ashamed of. It is how we deal with those things that makes us the males we are." In that moment, Oryon realized he had to confess to Isis what he had done. If he didn't, their entire future together would be based on an untruth that could destroy them.

"My Lord?" Jago asked, not knowing where his Lord's thoughts had gone.

"Things are going to be changing in House Rigel, Jago. My Isis is going to be involved in how our House is run from now on. She is going to be allowed to move freely in our House and on its grounds, but she is still going to need to be protected and that is where you come in."

"Me, my Lord?" Jago questioned.

"Yes. You are going to be the Captain of my Lady's Guard," Oryon told him.

"Me!" Jago skidded to a stunned halt beside his Lord.

"You," Oryon repeated, turning to look at the male. "It is not going to be an easy task I am assigning you. There are going to be many who are going to criticize your actions. You are going to be doing something no male on Betelgeuse ever has and that includes me. You are going to interact daily with a female that you are not Joined with. You will need to contact Warrior Agee, Captain of Queen Lisa's Guard, and ask his advice. He will have invaluable insight in what it takes to guard a demanding female, and have no doubt, Jago, my Isis is going to be demanding."

"I... my Lord... I am honored."

"We'll see how *honored* you feel when your actions are not only questioned by me, but by my male offspring, who, believe me, are going to be watching you closely."

"Will they have the right to overrule me?" Jago asked.

"No. When it comes to my Isis' safety, the only one that can overrule you is me."

"Including Ull?" Jago pressed, knowing as the future Lord, Ull would feel he had the right to.

"Including Ull," Oryon vowed.

"Then I will have no problem in dealing with them, my Lord."

Oryon smiled at Jago's confidence. The male had come a long way from the lost warrior that had presented himself to Oryon for training. He was now a warrior who Oryon was proud to say was from his House."

"My Lord..."

The suddenly concerned look on Jago's face had Oryon frowning. "What?"

"Smoke." Jago pointed behind Oryon. "Coming from House Rigel!"

Spinning on his heel, Oryon scanned the area where Jago had pointed. There, just the thinnest trail of smoke came from a place it never should have been.

"Isis..." Oryon whispered, then took off running toward his House.

∞ ∞ ∞ ∞ ∞

Kaspar moved quickly through the halls of House Rigel, nodding to those who passed as though nothing were wrong. Those that saw him would believe he was heading to his chamber. As Master of House Rigel, he had his own chamber on the upper level of the Warrior's Wing. He already knew he would not be going there. He had nothing there his credits couldn't replace. He was actually heading to the door that gave males access to the old training fields. From there he would make his way through the forest until he reached Parmelee, the closest village to House Rigel. There he would be able to secure passage off Betelgeuse.

Hearing voices, Kaspar was about to ignore them. Then he suddenly recognized one as Vali's.

Daco' He didn't have time to deal with Oryon's second male. Vali would question what he was doing and he didn't have *that* much time. Soon the blaze he started would be discovered.

Ducking into a dark corner, Kaspar watched as Vali directed four of Kaspar's own males who were carrying furniture. Furniture!

Furniture was what had caused this problem! That and the fact that a *female* had discovered what he was doing with that furniture. If he had the time, he would make her pay for that.

Waiting until he was sure he wouldn't be seen, Kaspar headed back the other way, toward the Common Wing of House Rigel, deciding he would use the door in the kitchen to make his escape. It would take him a little longer to disappear, but there was still time.

∞ ∞ ∞ ∞ ∞

"What are you doing in my kitchen?!!" Lajos demanded, seeing Kaspar enter during the busiest time of Lajos' day. Lajos didn't like Kaspar. He might run House Rigel but he didn't run the kitchen. Lajos ran the kitchen and he allowed *no one* to disrupt it right before a meal was served.

"I am here because I wish to be!" Kaspar fired back, refusing to back down, even now. As far as Lagos knew, Kaspar was still the Master of House Rigel.

"No one interferes in my kitchen before a meal! *Now get out!*" Lagos pointed toward the door.

Since Lagos was pointing to where Kaspar wanted to go, he said nothing, just glared at the male. Moving toward the door, a bag over his shoulder, heavy with his ill-gotten credits, he bumped into one of the kitchen trainees, knocking the bowl he carried to the floor.

"Galal!" Lajos screamed at the young male.

"I'm sorry Warrior Lajos. I did not see him," Galal stuttered, dropping to his knees to clean up the mess.

"You unfit male!" Kaspar spat at Galal. "You will never become a warrior fit enough to serve this House if you can't even control a bowl!" Flinging those hate-filled words at Galal, Kaspar headed out the door and to freedom.

∞ ∞ ∞ ∞ ∞

Isis made a slow, tight circle in the room that had once held so many memories for her. Now it was empty. Smiling, she hugged herself. She had done it! She had actually done it! She had been able to move beyond the restraints that had once been placed on her, and in doing so, discovered the female she was truly meant to be.

She couldn't wait to empty the rest of this floor and spread it throughout Rigel. Vali had been amazed by what he had seen in just this one room, what would he think when he saw the rest?

Walking into what was once her 'private' chamber, she looked at the things there. Most were items Oryon had given her, some she liked... others... not so much, but she had always treasured that *he* had thought to give them to her. Grabbing the ones she most cherished, she headed back down taking them to their new home.

She took her time selecting the perfect spot for each item. A beautiful piece of glass would sit on the windowsill, capturing the light and sending shards of color throughout the room. Oryon had given it to her after she had presented Ull.

She placed a stone sculpture of a warrior, his sword raised, ready to strike on the mantle. This was a piece Isis had never really liked. The warrior's expression was too stark, too unemotional. It was as if it didn't bother him that his strike was about to kill. Oryon had given it to her during their first year of Joining, shortly after the death of his manno, making him Lord.

Her first instinct had been to refuse it, letting him know it wasn't something she liked. Then Oryon had told her about it how it always went to the Lord's first male, the future Lord. It was meant to remind the male that if he were to be a successful Lord, he needed to remain strong and vigilant. Oryon's manno had only given it to him moments before his death, even though his brother had been dead for years.

Isis found she couldn't refuse the gift after that. She was ashamed to admit she had been relieved Oryon's manno had died. She had never liked the male. He had always seen Oryon as a lesser male than his brother. It was something Isis never understood because to her Oryon was *everything* a Lord should be and he wasn't anything like this cold, stone warrior. Turning it ever so slightly, Isis turned away, knowing exactly where she wanted to place the last piece she'd brought down.

Between the two large windows sat Oryon's desk. It was a large desk, with several levels that were full of little cubbyholes for him to store things. Some had doors and some didn't. Walking over to it, she let her fingers trail along its smooth surface, enjoying its silky feel. This was the private desk of a Lord. There were papers scattered across its wide surface, notes on training schedules, and reminders of things he needed to do.

Her manno's desk had been like this, full of things that needed his attention, things he wanted to do. It made her smile slightly to realize the two most important males in her life had so much in common and she hadn't even realized it.

Well now, they would have one more thing in common. Leaning forward, she placed the ancient carving of the Goddess on the top of Oryon's desk, centering it so the Goddess appeared to be gazing lovingly down at whoever was sitting there.

In truth, she was gazing at the tiny offspring she held in her arms. Isis' manno had told her how it had been in their bloodline since before the great infection and that it was believed to bless the male it was given to with female offspring. His own manno had been gifted with a female after Geb's presentation and while Isis had never met the female, her manno had spoken fondly of her.

Isis had prayed nightly to this intricate carving. At first, she had prayed that the Goddess would allow her to give Oryon female offspring, something deep in her heart she still wished for. Later, as the offspring the Goddess *had* blessed her with grew, her prayers had changed. She had begun to pray for the Goddess to provide *them* with females instead of herself.

Bowing her head, Isis thanked the Goddess for all the blessings she had bestowed on her males and asked for her assistance in helping Ull to find his way. Turning, she brushed several papers with her sleeve, scattering them across the floor.

Shaking her head, Isis dropped to her knees, gathering up the papers. As she was about to rise, she saw one that had slipped all the way under the desk. Crawling all the way under the desk, she finally reached the stray paper and began to back out. Thinking she was clear, Isis started to rise and hit the back of her head on the edge of the desk.

"Ouch!" She reached up to rub the small bump that was forming. When she did, her hand bumped a small vial out of its hiding spot under the desk. It rolled across the floor, stopping only when it ran into the newly placed rug.

Slowly, Isis reached up and blindly dropped the papers back on the desk. Her gaze never left the vial.

What was it?

Why was Oryon hiding it?

Still on her hands and knees, Isis cautiously crawled toward the vial as if it were as deadly as a wild termagant. She carefully picked it up between two fingers and heard a slight rattle from whatever was inside.

Hesitantly, she twisted off the top of the vial and poured whatever was inside into her waiting palm. Tablets... small blue tablets... Lifting one, she touched it to her tongue, then jerked back in shock.

Cohosh Gorm! An herb that when used in extremely small amounts could help stomach problems, in a tablet like this... Isis' mind flew. She knew this for some reason... why... her mother... her mother had told her that concentrated cohosh gorm... Isis' eyes widened in shock. Prevented conceiving!

Why did Oryon have *this*?

Rising to her feet, Isis went to find out.

∞ ∞ ∞ ∞ ∞

"Get back on your comm, Jago!" Oryon ordered over his shoulder, his eyes never leaving the darkening smoke. He had heard no alarm sounding, and that let him know the fire had not yet been discovered. "Contact Shen about the fire. Tell him we are en route and that I want the entire House secured, especially Isis." Oryon wasn't sure what he was sensing, but something was very wrong here, and he needed to make sure his Isis was safe.

"Yes, my Lord," Jago grunted, pulling out his comm. He had always known that his Lord was a fit male, but he was at least twenty years older than Jago, and Jago was having trouble keeping up with him. As Shen answered Jago's call, an explosion ripped through House Rigel, shattering windows.

∞ ∞ ∞ ∞ ∞

Kaspar smiled as he jogged up the rise. He had made it. He was free. No more would he have to serve a Lord that allowed a *female* to rule his House. Now *he* would be able to obtain a female. Cresting the rise, he skidded to a halt, for coming toward him at a dead run was Oryon himself, followed closely by Jago.

Realizing they had not yet seen him, Kaspar spun around and quickly retraced his steps back to House Rigel's kitchen.

"I told you to *get*..." An explosion cut off the rest of Lajos words, shaking the walls of House Rigel. Pots and Pans rattled and plates fell from shelves.

Every male in the kitchen froze, their eyes flying to Lajos.

"Secure the kitchen!" Lajos immediately ordered. "Shut down *everything*! Every stove! Every oven!"

"But the meal..." someone dared ask.

"Will wait!" Lajos spat out, his gaze spearing the male stupid enough to question him. He glanced back to Kaspar, expecting him to take control of the situation, and found him gone.

∞ ∞ ∞ ∞ ∞

"Here, Warrior Vali?" Jael asked stepping back from where they had set the chair.

"Yes. Thank you." Walking over to the chair his mother had given him, Vali couldn't stop his hand from running along the wood on top of its high back.

"It is a magnificent chair." Jael found himself saying, then lowered his eyes as Vali's gaze turned to him. "My apologies, Warrior Vali."

"Why are you apologizing? You are speaking truth."

"Yes, but I have not yet earned the right to speak to a warrior," he said quietly.

"Who has told you this?" Vali demanded. This was wrong. As long as a trainee showed respect, he was allowed to speak to whomever he liked.

"Master Kasper," Jael admitted to Vali.

"He is wrong, Jael." Vali waited, but when Jael said nothing and his eyes remained lowered, Vali realized there was more wrong here than he had thought. "Look at me Jael!"

Jael's gaze immediately flew to Vali.

"I do not know what Master Kaspar has been teaching you, any of you," Vali's eyes traveled over the other three trainees in the room. "But you have the right to speak to any male you wish, as long as you show him respect. How else are you expected to learn from him?"

"I..." Jael looked to his friends.

"Speak freely Jael," Vali ordered.

"Warrior Kaspar assured us he would not allow us to continue with our training if we did not do as he said. That Lord Oryon always agreed with his recommendations after his training."

Vali couldn't believe Jael actually believed this. "Do you truly believe your Lord, a male worthy enough to have a female remain with him his entire life, would *blindly* follow *any* male's recommendation?"

"I..." Jael's eyes widened. "No, my... Warrior Vali... my Lord, would never do that."

"Good, then it is understood that you may speak to warriors, and *I* will speak to Warrior Kaspar about..." An explosion drowned out the rest of Vali's words.

∞ ∞ ∞ ∞ ∞

Isis jerked open the outer doors of the Lord's Wing, startling the two warriors guarding the door. As she opened her mouth to demand to know where their Lord was, an explosion ripped through the House. Immediately, both males reached for their comms that were suddenly squawking.

Isis recognized the voice of Oryon's Captain through the comm, ordering House Rigel be secured and every male to the Common Wing to fight the fire. Static broke up the rest of his order.

"Go!" Isis ordered the two, who were looking at each in a panic.

"But my Lady!"

"You heard the Captain. He needs every male!"

"You will be unprotected!"

"House Rigel is being secured as we speak! Go! Make sure there is a House left to secure! I will be fine!" Spinning around on her heel, Isis reentered the Lord's Wing and slammed the door shut behind her.

∞ ∞ ∞ ∞ ∞

Kaspar rushed through the kitchen, uncaring what anyone thought. If Oryon caught up with him, Kaspar knew his life would be ended, for not only had he stolen from his Lord, but he had also attacked Oryon's House by setting that fire.

He needed to get away, but how? Shen's order came over the comms, calling for every male to converge in the Common Wing. Already the Warrior's Wing was emptying, every male rushing to obey Shen's order. If he went that way, it would raise the suspicions of every male.

If he stayed in the Common Wing, Oryon would find him. That left him only one means of escape, the Lord's Wing.

Turning on his heel, Kaspar ignored the young male he knocked down and took off at a run.

∞ ∞ ∞ ∞ ∞

Oryon burst through the kitchen door. He knew exactly where he needed to go. He had seen the flames shooting out of Kaspar's office windows on his way in. What in the name of the Goddess was going on?

"Lajos! Is your kitchen secure?!!" he demanded.

"Yes my Lord!" Lajos quickly informed him, "and I have sent my males to assist Captain Shen as ordered."

Nodding, Oryon stormed through the kitchen. He headed for the stairs that lead to the second level of the Common Wing and Kaspar's office.

Thick smoke billowed out of the corridor as Oryon and Jago charged down it. Trainees and warriors alike were working together to fight back the flames that were trying to take hold in House Rigel. Many had grabbed containers of flame repellant, while others where stomping out the small flames with their feet.

The flames in the hall were quickly extinguished, giving them access to the source, Kaspar's office. Inside, the room was fully engulfed, the flames being fed by the amount of adhmad in the room and the air surging through the shattered windows. If they didn't get it under control soon, it could destroy this entire wing of Rigel.

∞ ∞ ∞ ∞ ∞

Kaspar couldn't believe his luck. It had taken him some time, but he had been able to make it to the Lord's Wing unseen. Even the warriors that normally guarded the main doors had gone to assist in fighting the fire he had started. He had not planned on the explosion, having forgotten about the buama he had hidden away in a cabinet. It was normally a very stable substance but when exposed to high temperatures it exploded.

While it wasn't what he planned, it had turned out to be a blessing from the Goddess, for it cleared the path for his escape. Pushing open the outer door to Oryon's chambers, he slipped inside. Now all he needed to do was slip out one of the first floor windows and he could disappear.

"Oryon? Is that you?"

At the female's voice, Kaspar pivoted around.

Chapter Seven

Isis had been pacing ever since the guards left.

What was going on?

What had exploded?

Was anyone hurt?

Should she go find out?

Where was Oryon?

She couldn't remember the last time she had been this distraught and indecisive. She had gone to the windows facing the Common Wing and seen the thick black, smoke that billowed out several windows and the greedy flames that licked at the sides of her home.

Males came running from the training grounds, many raced into the wing to assist in putting out the flames, while others fought it from the outside, making sure the flames didn't spread to the Lord's Wing.

Hearing the outer door open, she rushed from their resting chamber. "Oryon? Is that you?" she asked before coming to an abrupt stop when she saw who had entered the chamber. "Kaspar. What are you doing here?"

Kaspar couldn't believe it. What was *she* doing here, on *this* level? She didn't belong here. She should have left House Rigel years ago. If she had, he would have been able to attract a female. Everything he had had to do today was *her* fault! She needed to *pay* for that.

"Kaspar, answer me, what are you doing here?" Isis refused to let the male see he intimidated her. This was *her* House. This was *her* Chamber. *He* had no right to be here without permission.

Kaspar growled at her words and moved toward her. Did she really think she could order *him* around? *Him*? *He* was Master of House Rigel! She was just a female, one that needed to be taught a lesson.

Isis took a startled step back at Kaspar's growl. No male had ever growled so menacingly at her like that before. None had ever moved toward her as if they wanted to harm her. Suddenly, she realized Kaspar *did* want to harm her. Before she could turn and run, he grabbed her in a bruising grip.

"You think you can talk to *me* like that?" He shook her hard. "*I* am a Tornian warrior! *I* am Master of House Rigel! *You* are nothing but a *female* and an *inferior* one at that."

"*Inferior!*" Isis found she couldn't cower before this male, couldn't stop herself from responding. "*I* have given my Lord *four* fit and worthy males!"

"You *stupid* female!" Kaspar pulled her to her toes as he spat at her. "You should have been giving that offspring to *other* males, males like *me! You* are the reason our Empire is declining."

"No!" Isis spat back. "It is because of *unfit* and *unworthy* males like *you*!"

"You *bitch*!" Lifting her off her feet, Kaspar threw her across the room.

Crying out in pain, Isis hit the wall and her world went black.

∞ ∞ ∞ ∞ ∞

It had taken some time, but they had finally gotten the fire out, had kept it from spreading. Stepping into the still smoldering room, Oryon inspected the damage and found most of it was concentrated where Kaspar's desk should have been.

"This was intentionally started," Oryon said to no one in particular.

"Agreed." Ull strode up next to his manno, his face streaked with soot. "But the question is why? And who?"

"Kaspar," Vali growled out, stepping next to his brother, the rims of his eyes darker then the soot covering him, "because of what mother discovered."

"What?" Ull's looked to Vali. "What are you talking about?"

"Mother discovered Kaspar was allowing substandard furniture into House Rigel."

"Not allowing, ordering," Oryon told them.

"What?!!" Both of them exclaimed.

"I've spoken to Master Bard myself, seen his invoices, and I would guess," Oryon's looked back to what remained of Kaspar's desk. "That the fire was started with Kaspar's falsified invoices."

"That son of Daco!" Ull spat out.

"Yes, and I'm sure he is long gone by now." Oryon agreed.

"He was still in the House after the explosion." All heads turned to Zev whose normally sparkling eyes were unusually serious. "He ran into me outside the kitchen and was heading for your wing."

"Towards *my* wing!" Oryon exclaimed.

"Yes, he was carrying a bag and knocked me down. I thought it was strange, but then I forgot about it once I got here. I'm sorry manno."

"It is not your fault. You did not know," Oryon reassured him. "Your mother will be fine. Mahir and Malden are guarding the door."

"Mahir and Malden..." Zev frowned at his manno, his gaze traveling behind him. "They are right there." He pointed.

"What!" Oryon spun around to find the two warriors in question standing by the window.

"Mahir! Malden!"

Oryon's shout had both males jumping, and then rushing to their Lord's side. "My Lord?"

"Why are you here?"

"My Lord?" Mahir and Malden looked at him in confusion.

"Who is guarding my Isis?" Oryon demanded.

"My Lord, Captain Shen ordered all males to the Common Wing!"

"Except those that were protecting my Isis!"

"My Lord that was not the orders we received, and when Lady Isis heard the House was being secured, *she* ordered us here to make sure there was a House left to secure."

"Of all the...." Oryon cut off his next words. That feeling that something was wrong returned with a vengeance. "Shen! Secure this area! The rest of you." He looked to his offspring. "You are with me."

"Yes, my Lord." Shen was talking to empty space for the males of House Rigel were gone.

∞ ∞ ∞ ∞ ∞

Oryon shoved males out of his way as he stormed out of the Common Wing. He needed to get to his Isis, needed to get to her *now*! He needed to make sure she was safe. Kaspar had been willing to burn down House Rigel to try to hide his crimes. If Isis came between him and his freedom, there was no telling what that unfit male might do to her.

Oryon held up his hand as they approached the closed doors of his wing, signaling his males to slow. They couldn't just run blindly in. They did not know the situation yet. If Kaspar was still in there, he might harm Isis.

Oryon was reaching for the handle when he heard Isis cry out, followed by the sound of something hitting a wall. Uncaring that he didn't even have his sword, Oryon threw open the door and rushed in.

∞ ∞ ∞ ∞ ∞

Kaspar smiled as Isis collapsed into a heap on the floor. *Now that's how you treat a female.* he thought then looked around the room. He had time. Maybe he should make use of her before he left. *That* would show *Lord* Oryon just who truly was the fittest warrior. As he took a step toward her, the Chamber door burst open and Oryon charged toward him.

Heart pounding with fear, Oryon spied Isis crumpled on the floor, unconscious, with Kaspar advancing on her. The rage that filled Oryon went beyond anything he had ever felt in his life, and he launched himself at the other male.

Kaspar stumbled back under the furious onslaught of Oryon's attack. He tried to protect himself from the punishing blows the older male was delivering, but for each one he blocked, two more seemed to land, the last one sending Kaspar to his knees. Looking up at his Lord, Kaspar was ready to plead for mercy, but never got the chance as Oryon punched him directly in the throat, crushing his windpipe.

Unemotionally, Oryon stared down at the male he had just given a deathblow to. Kaspar lay at his feet, his fingers clawing at his neck, trying to draw a breath from a throat that no longer existed. His eyes pleaded with Oryon's for a mercy that Oryon would never give.

"Manno!" Vali's call had Oryon turning his back on the dying male and rushing to his Isis' side.

∞ ∞ ∞ ∞ ∞

Isis fought to find her way out of the fog that seemed determined to blind her to where she was going. Up ahead was a faint light trying to guide her, but the fog kept trying to block it.

"Keep coming," a melodic voice encouraged, startling Isis, "if you want the life you have always prayed for."

"What?" Isis asked, her eyes searching for the voice, but was only answered by the fog thickening.

"Hurry," the voice said again, "or lose it all."

Isis didn't know what the voice was talking about, but she knew she didn't want to lose what she had fought so hard for. So trusting the voice, she ran toward the light that became brighter the closer she got. Finally after what seemed like an eternity, the fog finally released her and she was surrounded with the most amazing light.

"It took you long enough, child," the voice said.

Looking around, Isis found the source of the 'voice'. Dropping to her knees, she bowed her head. "Goddess," Isis whispered reverently.

"Rise child," the Goddess said, extending her hand to assist her.

After a moment's hesitation, Isis slipped her hand into the Goddess' and amazing warmth filled her. Everything was suddenly crisp and clear, there were colors she had never seen before and scents she had never smelled, yet every one comforted her.

"As you have comforted me for many years, you were the only one that gave me hope Isis."

"Hope?" Isis gave her a confused look.

"Yes that the Tornian people were worth saving."

"I..." Isis didn't know what to say. What could she have done to draw the attention of the Goddess?

"You refused to leave the male of your choice, even though many condemned you for it," the Goddess informed her.

"How could I have left him?" Isis asked. "It would have destroyed me to Join with another."

"As it did your mother," the Goddess looked at her with knowing eyes. "She had very strong feelings for your manno and I had hopes, but she allowed herself to be lulled away by 'things.'" The Goddess spat the word 'things' out as if it left a bad taste in her mouth.

"Her manno influenced her greatly." Isis didn't know why she was defending her mother, but she knew, while her manno had never forgiven her, he had continued to have strong feelings for her.

"For his own gain," the Goddess told her.

"He gained from her leaving my manno?"

"Of course." The Goddess' gazes softened. "You did not realize."

"No. Did my mother?"

"Only after it was too late," the Goddess informed her.

"That was why she became so bitter." Isis' mind traveled back to all the things her mother had said to her. How hard she had tried to get Isis to leave Oryon.

"Yes." The Goddess agreed.

"Did my manno know?"

"Yes."

"That was why he said he would always stand by me if I wanted to stay with just one male." Isis now had a better understanding of some of the things her manno had told her.

"Warrior Geb was a truly fit and worthy male."

"He was." Isis agreed knowing the amazing tribute the Goddess had just given her manno.

"You were my last hope, Isis," The Goddess quietly told her.

"Me?" Isis couldn't hide her surprise.

"Yes. If *you* had chosen another, if *Oryon* had forced you to give your gift to another, then I would abandon all hope for the Tornian people, but you didn't and he didn't. Because of *that*, I have allowed compatible females to be found."

"But..." Isis frowned at her.

"You question my decision?" the Goddess raised an eyebrow and the music ceased.

Isis looked at the Goddess. Only weeks ago she wouldn't have been brave enough to question the Goddess' actions. Now, because of the support and acceptance she had found from those who the Goddess called 'compatible' females, Isis found she had to. "Kim suffered."

"It was necessary..." the Goddess began and was shocked when she was cut off.

"No! It wasn't!" Isis ripped her hand way from the Goddess. "You are a Goddess! You could have prevented it! For you to just stand by and allow it, makes you no different than those that assisted Emperor Lucan!"

"How *dare* you!" The universe darkened in the presence of the Goddess' anger.

"I *dare* because it is truth!" Isis refused to back down. "Kim didn't need to suffer like that! To nearly *die*, for you to allow them to be found! You are the Goddess!"

Isis didn't know how long she was lost in the Goddess' eyes, it could have been minutes or it could have been years, but it seemed she saw all of creation in those turbulent gray eyes. Life and death, love and hate, sadness and joy, good and bad, all intermingled in such a way that they were nearly inseparable in the way they touched and blended, and Isis began to understand. "You can't have one without the other..." Isis whispered.

"No," the Goddess responded. "Each affects the other. What Lucan did... others should have stopped but didn't, and my rage caused these effects... I am responsible."

"Then fix it."

"I cannot 'fix' what *I* have caused. It is why a God or Goddess must use care in what prayers they answer. It is up to *you*, the ones I have harmed, to overcome what I have done."

"How can I do that?" Isis asked.

"*You* gave me hope that a Tornian female could still love a Tornian male. *Oryon* showed me that a Tornian male could love a Tornian female. Because of the two of you, I brought Kim here to find out if *this* Emperor was anything like Lucan and he has more than proven he is not. In doing so, I discovered there are more males that would be like Oryon and Wray if a female truly cared for *them*, if she loved and trusted in them, as they had in the past before what *I* did in anger changed that relationship forever."

Isis looked at the Goddess and saw the true regret that swam in her eyes. "What must we do?"

"What you are doing. What you have been doing. Stand by the one you love, no matter what. There will be difficult times ahead for you, Isis. Daco is not going to give up what he has gained because of my actions." The Goddess looked to the stars. "It is time for you to go. Your male is becoming very... impatient." Her gaze returned to Isis. "He loves you very much Isis. Remember that in the trials that are to come, and learn from my mistakes.

∞ ∞ ∞ ∞ ∞

"Why isn't she waking?!!" Oryon demanded of the Healer as he stared at his Isis from the side the bed. She was lying in the center of it so still and pale.

"I do not know, my Lord." The Healer frowned as he studied his scanner. "I can find no reason for it. The blow to the head was not that severe."

No longer able to remain so far from his Isis, Oryon sat beside her on the bed then leaned back on the headboard as he slid his arm under her to cradle her against his chest.

"My Lord, she shouldn't be moved!" the Healer protested.

"What she shouldn't *be* is *unconscious*!" Oryon growled at the Healer, and the look he gave the Healer told him not to speak again.

"Come Healer Asa." Vali's tone was mild, but his grip was firm, as he led the Healer away. "My manno knows what my mother requires."

"Wake Isis," Oryon whispered, ignoring everyone else in the room as he kissed her temple. "Wake for me, for my life is meaningless without you in it."

∞ ∞ ∞ ∞ ∞

Oryon's offspring watched and listened in amazement as their manno whispered to their mother. They had all known their relationship was unusual after all; they were the product of it. They had seen them together, especially on Tornian, but even with that, they had not understood the true depth of their manno's feelings for their mother. Not until they listened to his whispered words, and saw the tears that flowed freely down his cheeks.

Before them was a male they all looked up to, who they wanted to emulate, yet here he was saying his life meant nothing without the female in his arms. Was it truly possible? That a female could mean that much to a male? Did that weaken a male? Or strengthen him?

∞ ∞ ∞ ∞ ∞

Fog surrounded Isis again, only this time there was no light, no voice. No wait... there was a voice, but it wasn't the Goddess'. Who was it?

'*...my life is meaningless without you in it...*'

She knew that voice. Oryon! Without another thought, she flew to his voice for she knew without *him*, *she* was nothing.

"Oryon..."

Every male in the room froze at their mother's faint whisper, then watched in amazement as her eyes fluttered open, immediately searching for their manno.

"Why are you crying, my love?" Isis whispered reaching up to wipe away the tears that didn't belong on her male's face.

"I thought I had lost you." Oryon buried his face in the crook of her neck.

"You could never lose me," she vowed caressing his check. Suddenly, she realized they were not alone and her gaze flew to find her offspring watching them intently. She took in their disheveled state and it all came rushing back to her. "Kaspar! The fire!"

"Both are taken care of. There is nothing for you to concern yourself with," Oryon quickly reassured her. "You only need to rest."

"The fire is out? Everyone is safe?" Isis continued to question, her eyes rushing over her offspring, taking in their soot-covered clothing, searching for any injuries.

"Yes, as is our House and offspring." Oryon knew that was what her real fear was, that something had happened to their offspring. "Rest, Isis, I will be here when you wake."

As her hand came to rest over Oryon's heart, she let its steady beat reassure her, and she slept.

∞ ∞ ∞ ∞ ∞

When Isis woke, she was alone. Rolling over, she found that night had fallen outside the windows and someone had started a roaring fire in the room. Rising up, she could see trays of food waiting to be eaten on a low table before the couch. Everything seemed warm and inviting. But where was Oryon?

"I'm here," Oryon's steady voice came from the doorway separating the outer chamber from their resting chamber. "Ull needed direction in the cleanup and I didn't want to disturb you. I'm sorry I wasn't here when you woke." He quickly moved to her side, his eyes searching hers for the slightest hint of pain.

"I'm fine," she quickly reassured him, taking his arm so she could continue to rise. "What was Ull's problem?"

"He was concerned about the damage the fire did to the structure of the Common Wing," he told her absently, more concerned about making sure she was steady on her feet, than Ull.

"What did you tell him to do?" Isis asked.

"I told him to contact Master Bard. He will be able to direct him on what needs to be done and who is qualified to do it."

"Your Master Cabinetmaker?"

"Yes."

"You trust him? Even after he made that furniture?" Isis quizzed.

"He made what Kaspar ordered him to make. I have seen the invoices myself. His only failing is that he never verified them with me. Something, Kaspar assured him, would get him dismissed from my House. Kaspar blamed *you* for it being necessary."

"Me?" Isis looked at him shocked.

"Yes, Kaspar told Bard that your demands were putting a strain on our House's resources. Which was why I ordered peine instead of solid dair."

"And Bard believed him?"

"Unfortunately yes, but it has been corrected."

"Good, no male should ever be afraid to come speak to you. You are a fit and worthy Lord, Oryon."

"Thank you, my love. Now come, you need to eat. I had Cook send up several items for you to choose from."

It was only later, after they had eaten when Oryon rose to stoke the fire and Isis was leaning back on the couch that her hand brushed against the vial she had put in her pocket earlier.

"I want Asa to check you again before we rest, Isis." Oryon turned his back to the fire and found his Isis staring at him with a peculiar expression on her face.

"Is Asa the one who gave you this?" Isis held up the vial so it glimmered in the firelight.

"Gave me what?" Oryon took a step closer before coming to an abrupt halt, paling. "Where did you get that?" he whispered, his voice tight.

"It fell out from under your desk when I placed the statue of the Goddess on it. It's cohosh gorm." Isis' eyes darkened with betrayal as she looked at him. "Why?" she asked. "We talked about this after Ynyr was presented."

"And then you conceived Zev!" Oryon said with more force than he had intended. "You refused to allow your mother to attend to you and I nearly lost you during his presentation! I was not going to allow that to happen again!"

"That's not true!" Isis surged to her feet. "Yes, I had a difficult time with Zev but that was my own fault. I waited too long to notify Asa. Had I let him examine me while I was carrying Zev, as Lisa is now doing with Hadar, then it would have been easier."

"I was not going to take that chance!" Oryon refused to back down.

"That wasn't your decision! You know that I wanted to give you more offspring."

"And I wanted *you*!" Oryon ran angry fingers through his hair. "*Goddess*, Isis, you gave me four fit and worthy offspring before you were even thirty! Your body was telling you to stop! You wouldn't listen and do what was necessary to remain with me, so I did!"

"You let me think I had failed you."

"I never did!" He denied. "Not by word or deed!"

"I wanted to give you a female…" Isis whispered, her eyes filling.

"And we both know what would have happened if you had." Oryon told her, refusing to be swayed by her tears.

"I wouldn't have left you Oryon. No one could have made me do that."

Oryon moved to his chair, dropping down into it with a heavy sigh, rubbing his hands over his face roughly. "They would have just taken you Isis." He raised weary eyes to her. "They would have come and taken you."

"Who? Wray?" Isis refused to believe it.

"No, not Wray, his manno, there were already stirrings of discontent after Vali was presented. If I hadn't been a Lord…"

"He would have taken me from you?" Isis paled at the thought. "Forced me to Join with another?"

"Yes. He informed me that it was only because of my position and continued support for him that he didn't, but that if you gave me a female he would be forced too."

Isis sat on a low table across from Oryon, putting a gentle hand on his knee. "Why didn't you tell me?" she asked.

"Because I knew you would be willing to take the risk. I wasn't. I needed you in my life, Isis. Just the thought of another male…" Oryon's face darkened at the thought.

"You still shouldn't have kept this from me, especially with how things have changed."

"I know." He covered her hand with his and squeezed. "I realized that today after talking to Jago."

"To Jago?" Isis frowned wondering what Jago could have said to Oryon to get him to tell her.

"He wanted to be released from his vow because everyone now knew of the unfit decisions he had made in the past."

"But he overcame them. He broke his addiction to Whisk and regained his honor."

Her instance defense of him told Oryon she was as proud to have Jago in their House as he was. "Yes, he faced them and moved on. It was then that I realized I needed to do the same with you. I needed to tell you about the cohosh gorm and hoped you would forgive me. Will you Isis? Forgive me for wanting to keep you safe, for wanting to keep you with me and your offspring? For we would be lost without you."

Isis looked deep into her male's eyes and saw that he was honestly worried that she wouldn't forgive him. She thought back to the Goddess' plea that Isis needed to learn from *her* mistake of judging too quickly and harshly, and then not being able to correct it and she realized she didn't need the Goddess' advice.

There was nothing in the known universes that could cause her to leave her Oryon. Certainly not a deception that was only done with the best intentions, but she would make sure it never happened again.

"I would never leave you, Oryon. Haven't I proven that to you already? But," she said when he went to pull her into his arms, "I want your vow that nothing like this will ever happen again. I am your Lady and I have the right to know if I am being threatened, even if it is by the Emperor."

"I vow!" Oryon immediately stated.

Isis evaded his grip again. "And I want you to stop taking the cohosh gorm."

"What?" Oryon's eyes narrowed.

"I am forty-three years old Oryon, the chances of me still being able to conceive are slim. But I want to know that if I don't, that it is because it is the will of the Goddess, not because of a drug."

For several long moments Oryon just watched her, then he held out his hand, waiting.

Isis handed him the vial.

Oryon stood, then walked over to the fire. He tightly gripped the mantle with one hand while the other fisted the vial. "My vow." He Looked at her with hard eyes. "But I demand your vow in return. If it *is* the will of the Goddess that you conceive, then you will immediately see Healer Asa and the Healer

Rebecca. You will do whatever they tell you. No matter what! I cannot lose you Isis!"

Isis opened her mouth to argue, then realized she could not. She would be demanding the same thing if somehow the situation was reversed.

"My vow." She crossed the room to his side. "And you will *never* lose me, because I will always be here," she said placing her hand over his heart.

Covering her hand with his, Oryon threw the vial into the fire and placed their future into the hands of the Goddess and prayed she would be merciful.

Epilogue

"Are you going to be?" The whispered words, so close to her ear sent a shiver of excitement through the Goddess as her mate's arms encircled her, pulling her back against his hard frame.

"Going to be what?" she asked softly sinking into his embrace.

"Be merciful." Kissing her shoulder, he looked down at the couple she had been watching so intently. "They have always been two of your favorites."

"Yes, they have been, and yes, I'm going to be. Perhaps more so than either expects." The Goddess smiled as the idea grew. "Oh yes, I'm going to be *very* merciful."

"Hmm, well I think you should show *your* mate some mercy first. Come *rest* with me my love," he coaxed, and laughing the Goddess allowed herself to be led away.

About the Author

Michelle has always loved to read and writing is just a natural extension of this for her. Growing up she always loved to extend the stories of books she'd read, just to see where the characters went. Happily married for over twenty-five years she is the mother of two amazing children. You can reach her at m.k.eidem@live.com or her website at http://www.mkeidem.com she'd love to hear your comments.